The Young Druids

To Kirsty
Best Wishes
Gwyn Morgan
x

The Young Druids

Powers and Spirits

GWYN MORGAN

Copyright © 2014 by Gwyn Morgan.

ISBN: Softcover   978-1-4931-9422-3
           eBook   978-1-4931-9423-0

All rights reserved. No part of this book may be reproduced or transmitted in any form or by any means, electronic or mechanical, including photocopying, recording, or by any information storage and retrieval system, without permission in writing from the copyright owner.

This is a work of fiction. Names, characters, places and incidents either are the product of the author's imagination or are used fictitiously, and any resemblance to any actual persons, living or dead, events, or locales is entirely coincidental.

Any people depicted in stock imagery provided by Thinkstock are models, and such images are being used for illustrative purposes only.
Certain stock imagery © Thinkstock.

This book was printed in the United States of America.

Rev. date: 04/29/2014

To order additional copies of this book, contact:
Xlibris LLC
0-800-056-3182
www.xlibrispublishing.co.uk
Orders@xlibrispublishing.co.uk
619945

Chapter 1

At first it was just the eyes. Pale blue as old as ice and curiously intense, they seemed to be staring into Alwyn's very soul. Countless times now they had woken the boy from his sleep in a cold sweat. He had told no-one, afraid he was going mad, but the training he was undergoing from the team of knowledgable, elderly Druids was beginning to take effect. Often enough he had been told that he possessed that rare power of controlling his dreams and that his dreams had a reality denied to most of the human race. Alwyn began to shake off his fear and bring the power of his mind to bear on those dreadful eyes, and slowly he began to see more. In time, he saw a face, thin and hard, of a man in middle years with long straight hair the colour of an iron blade, a short grey beard that did nothing to disguise high, sharp cheekbones and thin, bloodless lips turned down in disapproval. Shivering slightly, Alwyn turned his mind back to those eyes and stared back into them, as if to see into the soul beyond them. At once he saw a change, a narrowing of the eyes, a look of disbelief, for a moment, even a touch of fear which turned instantly into a look of such pure hate that the young boy opened his own eyes with a start. Shaking with shock, Alwyn realised immediately that he had not been experiencing recurring dreams, but those frightening eyes were real. Somewhere a man with terrifying powers was trying, and in some senses succeeding, in staring into his very mind. Furthermore, this person now knew that Alwyn too, had powers of the mind, undeveloped as yet, but capable of staring back at the intrusive stranger. Whoever it was, now had reason to fear Alwyn and the boy was sure, hate him.

Myrthin, Head Druid of the Island of Britain looked worried as he listened to Alwyn's tale. His brows knitted together as he ran his thin fingers through his long, silky white beard. The old man's eyes flicked over Alwyn's shoulders to the grizzled face of Ceriod, the boy's chief tutor and Myrthin's most trusted adviser. Ceriod looked every bit as anxious as his illustrious leader and his wise old eyes opened as he gave the Head Druid an almost imperceptible nod. Myrthin spoke quietly, but his rich, deep voice seemed to flow over Alwyn like honey.

'Well, boy, Elder Ceriod speaks well of your character and your developing powers, and you are going to need both indeed in the time to come. You are right in surmising that that the eyes and face you saw so clearly are real. By your description they are the eyes and face of the Lord Maelgwyn. He was a Druid, here on the island of Mona. He has immense powers and was destined for great things but he became greedy, impatient, unwilling to use those great powers solely for the benefit of all the peoples of the Island of Britain. Above all, we discovered that he was prepared to use his powers for things more worldly than the pursuit of Truth. He broke the circles that must bind all of us who are called to serve as Druids and he was therefore expelled. He travelled back to his home territory, in the mountains, not thirty miles from here and used his powers to cow the local people and create himself a lordship of sorts. In many ways he is little more than a brigand chief, but with one great difference, he has powers, that were it not for the combined strength of the Druids here on Mona, he would use for great evil'

Shocked by the words of the great man, and greatly in awe of him, despite his well known kindness, Alwyn somehow found the courage to gulp and ask the questions he knew he must ask.

'But Lord Myrthin, why was he looking at me? How does he even know I exist? What does he want of me and why now does he seem angry with me?'

The old man smiled kindly, but Alwyn noticed, with some sadness.

'It seems that you remember very little of your early childhood Alwyn?"

Seeing the boy shake his head sadly, Myrthin continued. "As you have no doubt been told, you were born of poor famers far west of here in the lands of the Decanglii. It was and still is a land much plagued by pirate raids from Erin. One day, when you only about three, you told your parents that you knew the bad men were coming that day, and that the family should tell the neighbours and run away. Of course your parents ignored what they thought was infant nonsense, but sure enough, there was a raid that day and many villagers were killed. Your parents, having no familiarity with such powers, were terrified by what others would think, but they told the village headman. He saw the potential to raise his influence with the local king, who sent his court Druid to investigate. That Druid, unfortunately, was Maelgwyn. He took you away from your parents, telling them that you would be educated as a Druid on Mona. In fact he took you to the hideaway in the hills he was preparing with his acolyte, Bran. He tried to enter your mind then, to see if he could use and control your powers. The mental scream of anguish you gave was heard by the adept all over Mona. We set out to find you and using our combined powers we discovered you and Maelgwyn. He was already under a warning for his misuse of his powers, and this was the final straw. He was exiled from Mona for life and and was banned from practising as a Druid. We tried to find your parents, but they were dead, killed by raiders or Bran, no-one could tell us. So, Alwyn, we brought you here and you were given into the care of Ceriod and his helpers. I expect that Maelgwyn, who is a great hater, blames you for his downfall. Now it seems he has heard of your progress young man. You must realise that in twenty five years since Maelgwyn first came here, no Druid has been found with powers to match his. Ceriod trained Maelgwyn as well as you, and he tells me that you have the potential to be a far greater Druid than Maelgwyn could ever have been. What is more important, he is sure that you have the character and goodness that Maelgwyn lacked, a commitment to serve the Truth.'

The Head Druid stopped speaking at this point and placed his hands on Alwyn's temples. The long supressed memories of those bad days of his infancy came flooding back and tears streamed down Alwyn's pale and youthful face. Myrthin stared tenderly at Alwyn as if to judge his reaction to these revalations. Alwyn could feel the heat rising in his face and used the mental control he had been taught to govern his breathing and blood flow.

'I thank you Lord Myrthin for those words. I will strive to live up to them. But after all these years what does this Lord Maelgwyn want with me now?'

Lord Myrthin looked across at Ceriod again and motioned him to check beyond the door.

'I have said this to very few people and none as young as you, but doubtless, with your powers you cannot be entirely ignorant of what I shall say. The Romans mean to destroy us, Alwyn. They fear our power amongst the peoples of Britain, Gaul, Iberia and further afield. If they can, they will use their military might to wipe us out. I have a number of plans in place to prevent this, but all the seers tell me that Mona as a place of learning and Truth is doomed. Ah! I see from your eyes that you too have dreamed some at least of that dream. Maelgwyn, above all others will have seen that dream too. He alone will exult in it. He knows that only by our collective efforts have we curtailed his power, and will believe that if the power of Mona is ended then nothing can stop him using his powers to extend his wealth and influence. He does not fear the Romans because he knows he can use them to achieve his aims. Then, my boy, he hears tell of the young Druid with potential powers that could threaten him, the very boy who he blames for his fall from grace. He has looked into your mind and soul and then, to his horror he has found you looking back! Now he knows he is facing someone who, if he does nothing, will threaten his plans. He cannot wait and hope that the Romans will do the job for him. No, Alwyn, he will try to kill you and soon!'

The Head Druid's words, spoken quietly at first then with increasing power until the very sound seemed to be vibrating through his bones, shocked Alwyn deeply. He had indeed had those dreams where he saw thousands of Roman soldiers marching up the beaches from the Straits. He had seen the Druids, men and women sending out their curses and imprecations, the warriors with their long swords and bright cloaks all being ground into the mud under the nailed boots of the invaders, but he had not dared believe his own dreams. Surely nothing in the world was more powerful than the Truth, and who but the Druids could interpret and control it? On top of all this, there was now this new and dangerous adversary, Lord Maelgwyn of the chilling eyes, who meant to kill him because of powers he barely understood yet, let alone fully controlled. Nevertheless, Alwyn used what he had learned, and in a voice still shaking with emotion he spoke.

'Lord Myrthin, I am ready to do whatever you command, use my powers, such as they are, in whatever way you see fit, the Truth must be served and protected'

The old man smiled sadly

'Bravely spoken boy. I see that Ceriod has judged you aright. Yes, I have prepared certain plans for this eventuality. I had hoped to have a few months more to ready them, but I see now that I must bring them forward. In two weeks Alwyn, you must leave Mona in the company of some others who will protect you and indeed, you will protect them as well. You must travel to two of the the most sacred places in the Island of Britain, the Carn of Spirits and Ynys Avalon where you, and some other youngsters of great potential can meet with some great Druids who can release the full potential of your powers and prepare you in how to use them as Druids. From each of these two places you must also take an object of great significance to our culture; the Golden Torc of Aneurin, the first Head Druid; and the Bronze Cauldron of Erin that was was won from the King of Erin by King Bran in the distant past. Neither of these priceless relics must fall into the hands of Maelgwyn or the Romans, so you must take them to Erin to be cared for by the Druids there. If the Seers are correct, you may be amongst the last of us, and your other task will be to see that the Truth is remembered and learned by others for generations to come. This is an onerous task for one so young, but Alwyn, I believe in your destiny, and I will ensure that you are as prepared for your quest as possible. You will not be alone, and remember this, nothing is more powerful than the Truth and you have it in your armoury, and you enemies do not. I know you will face great dangers, but you will succeed. Go back to your room now young man and Ceriod will give you something to help you sleep. Tomorrow your preparations will begin'

These last words were delivered with such tender gentleness that Alwyn, despite the shocking task laid upon him, felt calm and almost ready to sleep and was led from the room by Ceriod. Myrthin sadly watched him go for a moment, then stood up with surprising speed in one so old and quietly said the name 'Lorchar!' A slender woman in her thirties dressed all in black appeared from behind a curtain and whispered 'My Lord?' The Head Druid looked at the woman with some sadness in his eyes

'Lorchar my dear, you know what to do. Begin the preparations!' With a brief nod, the woman left, Myrthin sat down again and put his head in both his hands.

Chapter 2

The late afternoon sun blazed down on the dusty hillside and the day's exertions had been made even harder by the unaccustomed heat. No doubt all the warriors practising their war skills on the open grasslands were tired, but none of them felt it as keenly as Owain, as he wiped the dust and sweat from his eyes and leant on his shield to regain his breath. He was sixty years old now and was only too aware that even the most grizzled veterans before him were at least fifteen years younger than him. For the last hour, only his pride had sustained him as he battled up and down these hills with energetic young men, a third his age, determined to boast in their drink that evening, that they had bested Owain the Gladiator in a fight, albeit a practice battle. Was he getting too old for this task of training the warriors who would protect the Druids of Mona from the dreaded Romans? The moment needed a deed, and with an earth shaking yell, Owain bent down, picked a vast rock from the ground, and with a grunt of effort lifted it high in the air and kept it there. Warriors all over the hillside stopped their training, and, in silence at first, but followed soon with laughter and cheers, applauded their famous war leader. Why fear the Romans while they had Owain the Gladiator to lead and train them? Owain saw the brief look of concern on the face of his son Garth. Seventeen years old and already the biggest and possibly the strongest warrior on Mona, perhaps even in the whole island of Britain, Owain's heart filled with pride in his son, who smiled broadly at his father as the grizzled old warrior threw down the great rock and shouted to the assembled men to go home now and rest, and not to drink too much as they had another day's practice tomorrow, and if they thought today's was hard . . . .

Perhaps only Garth knew how much each day's training cost Owain. The old man had kept himself fit, and his strength was still great, evidenced in the massive muscles of his shoulders and chest, but old wounds, and forty and more years of exertion now gave him much pain at the end of each day. Owain knew what he must do know to ease the pains and bring down the angry swelling in his joints. He watched the others make their way down the hill to the town, then he headed over the hill to the clear, swiftly running stream on the other side. After checking there was no-one about, Owain gave a little groan of exhaustion and pain, as he took off the short Roman style tunic and breeches he wore for fighting and training, and naked, lowered himself in the icy stream with a gasp as the cold water took his breath away. He had learned this technique to get rid of aches and pains many years ago, under his old Gladiator Master high in the hills of Southern Gaul, and it was still effective, though these days he had to stay in the water a little longer than was strictly comfortable. The old warrior closed his eyes, but then the peace was broken as a small but confident voice said

'A good method Master Owain, but I could prepare you an infusion that could help ease the pains for longer'

Before the sentence was finished Owain was out of the water, and the wickedly sharp Roman gladius was in his hand as he looked around for his surprise visitor.

Sitting on the bank, not five paces from him was a young girl with tawny hair and a green kirtle, perhaps twelve or thirteen years old. She seemed neither frightened by his angry appearance and sword, nor shocked by his nakedness. Suddenly aware of the foolishness of his situation, Owain angrily turned away from the girl, and muttering furiously to himself, pulled on a few clothes. He turned to face the girl again and seeing the smirk of amusement on the freckled, snub nosed face, he exclaimed

'Girl, I could have killed you then, what are doing here and where did you spring from? I checked the area and there is no cover!'

The girl raised her eyebrows and shrugged.

'Master Owain I was here before you arrived. People do not usually see me unless I wish them to. I have been watching you for a few days. I am a healer, and one does not usually see so many old wounds and swollen joints. It has been most instructive'

The normally equable old warrior was now black with fury.

'Girl, have some respect, you should not be hiding and watching your elders in secret. What gives you the right to do such things?'

Seeing the evident anger of the much respected war leader, the girl's attitude abruptly changed. The laughing eyes grew serious and she stood up and took a deep breath as if she was about to deliver a prepared speech.

'Honoured Sir' she began in a steady calm voice so different from the childlike insouciance of earlier. 'I apologise for observing you in secret and then surprising you in an embarrassing situation after your difficult day. Please allow me to explain myself. My Name is Branwen The Healer, daughter of Ceridwen the Healer, who lived in the great forest by the coast for many years. After my mother died two years ago I was brought to the town, and Lord Myrthin himself ordered that my care and education be entrusted to the Lady Lorchar, one of his closest advisers, as you may know. It was at the express instructions of the Lady Lorchar herself that I was instructed to watch you carefully to determine your health. The reason for this was not told to me, but I was told that it was at the wish of Lord Myrthin himself'

Suddenly this serious self assurance broke down and Branwen rushed to Owain and fell at his feet, grasping his ankles and sobbing.

'Master Owain, please do not tell Lord Myrthin or Lady Lorchar of my rudeness and indiscretion, they would be angered at my lack of respect to you, one of Lord Myrthin's oldest friends, and might not give me any new tasks to perform.'

Owain grinned at the change in the young girl and gently raised her to her feet. 'Well, young Branwen, a pretty apology and a well delivered speech, though I am perplexed at why Myrthin should be sending you out here to check on my health in secret. Perhaps he no longer has confidence in me' At this he shook his head in sad silence for a moment. Then he smiled again 'I am sorry that I was so angry, I suppose my pride was hurt that a young girl could hide from a veteran as experienced as me. But you know I did come very close to killing you in the instant reaction of a soldier caught off guard'

The girl's cheeky grin returned.

'Master you should not reproach yourself. I find that if I don't want to be seen, then no one will be able to find me, and as to killing me, even someone as skillful and strong as you would find that very difficult. I am sure you need have no doubts about the confidence that Lord Myrthin has in you, he talks of you with great affection. But Sir, I am charged to ask you if you will call on Lord Myrthin before the sun goes down this evening and sup with him. He has something important that he wishes to ask you. He asks if you will bring your son Garth with you.'

Owain looked puzzled again but told his young messenger that he and his son would be there as requested. He turned briefly to pick up his sword and shield, and when he turned back the girl was nowhere to be seen. Owain swore a long and disgusting gladiator's oath in Latin, and told himself that there was no such thing as the Fair Folk that all the peasants feared. He did not believe in magic and, despite his long and close friendship with the most important Druid in Britain, he was not even sure he believed in religion and the world of spirits. Therefore there must be a a perfectly logical explanation for the appearance and disappearance of Branwen the Healer, and he would doubtless ask Myrthin himself what that explanation was, once the great man had told Owain what all this cloak and dagger stuff was all about. Muttering all the while, Owain the Gladiator made his way down the hill.

Meanwhile, thirty or so miles away, in a secluded valley in the mountains of the mainland, Lord Maelgwyn was angrily trying to explain to his two perplexed chief advisers why all their plans now had to change.

'No! it is no use now expecting the Romans to do our job for us! The boy now knows that I am watching him and if he has half the ability I suspect, he will know that I am a real presence and a direct threat to him.

The boy is a protege of that tiresome prig Myrthin, and whatever else he may be, the man is not a fool. He now knows these indisputable facts. Firstly, the Romans are determined to destroy Mona as a centre for Druidic learning, and that pathetic little army he is building will not save the Druids of Mona from extermination. Secondly, without the combined power of the those Druids, there is little to stop me using my powers to gain wealth and influence in this part of Britain and, who knows, further afield. Thirdly, for the first time in a generation they have a young Druid with the potential power to stand in my way, given time and training. Now he knows that I am aware of his existence, and that I will seek either to destroy the boy or capture him and make use of his powers for my own ends. Mark my words, Myrthin will long have had a plan in place to spirit this boy away before the Romans come. Now he will not dare wait. Soon, in days, a couple of weeks, at most, an attempt will be made to get the boy off the island and take him to Druids living in seclusion elsewhere in Britain'

One of the two advisers spoke up. He was a tall, well built young man with the long bleached and stiffened hair favoured by young warriors. His handsome face was marred by a long scar down his cheekbone and his pale blue eyes blazed with fervour.

'Let me go to Mona tonight I will find where the boy is staying, and either kill him or capture him as you will my lord!'

Maelgwyn's laugh was loud and harsh.

'Your courage does you more credit than your brain my boy. You have no idea of the power of Druids even after all these years of working with me. They would be aware of your presence even before you landed on the island, and they would not use their warriors to oppose you. They would use their minds, and you would be returned to me like a helpless child!'

The young warrior bristled at this dismissal and was about to make an angry rejoinder when his companion stepped in. Tall and slim with long, glossy black hair and grey, intelligent eyes, Bran only ever spoke after considering all the options, and both the hotheaded young buck and furious ex Druid knew that what he said would be worth listening to.

'Of course my Lord, I may be wrong, but it seems to me that events may have played directly into our hands. As you so correctly point out, a direct assault to remove such a well protected young man would be out of the question, and we would have found it difficult to acertain exactly when Myrthin would have him taken off the island. Now we know it must be soon, and I dare to suggest that Myrthin will not attempt to send him off with a large armed guard or a group of powerful and well known Druids for protection. No, he will attempt to spirit the boy away in a small group, in disguise. So as not to raise suspicions, I would suspect a group no larger than, say ten people, possibly smaller They will rely on a swift, hidden escape rather than force or Druidic powers. All we need to do, using our supporters on the island, and some watchers along the coast, is to keep our eyes peeled for any groups leaving the island, follow them for a while, then intercept.'

Lord Maelgwyn, sitting by this time, was silent for a while as stroked his short beard, deep in contemplation. Then he spoke

'You are, as always, quite correct Bran, perhaps this is an opportunity after all. But we must beware of the subtlety and cunning of Lord Myrthin. He will be aware that we will be watching out for groups leaving the island, so what plans will he have made to deal with our possible discovery of the boy? Who can he send from Mona that would have the campaign skills to keep us from killing or capturing the boy? In my view, there is only Owain.'

At this, Cerrig, the bleached hothead warrior could restrain himself no more.

'What that fat old ex Gladiator? He could not last five minutes against me in battle! Besides, doesn't Myrthin need him to train that rabble of so called warriors they have, to meet the might of the Roman legions?'

Maelgwyn laughed, but it was not a pleasant or cheerful sound.

'True, Cerrig, but it may be that the old Druid has consulted with his seers and knows that the fight will be futile. In which case Owain's skills will be put to better use protecting the boy. By the way, be careful if you do come up against Owain in battle, he may indeed be rather long in the tooth these days, but he has learned more about fighting than you will ever learn, for all your courage and ferocity. I had the pleasure of seeing him in battle a few years ago, and believe me he had lost none of his strength and cunning. If you underestimate him it could be a fatal error'

Bran spoke up again before a flushed looking Cerrig could say something he might regret.

'So, with your permission my lord I will get word to our informants on the island and post sentries all long the coast to watch out for boats carrying a young man and some companions across the straights. If they send Owain the Gladiator with the boy he will at least be difficult to disguise. Within a month my lord we will have the boy or he will no longer be a threat to your plans.'

Lord Maelgwyn dismissed the two advisers with a wave of his hand, but when they were gone he remained seated, deep in thought, his mind kept flashing back to the day when Myrthin had arrived with his best men and had humiliated him. He hated Myrthin but knew he would soon be dead or a Roman prisoner. But the boy, the boy must either die or be his slave, a weapon he could use to advance his power.

Chapter 3

Sitting amongst the furs and padded hides of Lord Myrthin's hall were Owain, the Lady Lorchar, the old Druid Ceriod and Myrthin himself. They had eaten well and after the servant had filled the mead cups one last time and left, the Head Druid ceased the pleasantries that had taken up the last hour and and at last spoke of the issue all were there to discuss.

'Well Owain, old friend, you are not going to like what I am about to propose to you, but I hope you will take my word that it is crucial to the future of the Island of Britain and the maintenance of the Truth. However, I first need you to be brutally honest with me. If it is true that Governor Paulinus is on his way with three legions plus auxiliaries, what chance do we have of preventing their invasion of this island and the destruction of all we do here on Mona?'

Owain sat silent for a moment, rocked by the brutal bluntness of the question, then he set his jaw and replied without a waver in his voice.

'In truth Myrthin, there is no chance at all. Their invasion will be successful, and all who oppose it will die or be taken into slavery! The best we can hope for is to cost them very dear indeed, and weaken them if there should be uprisings elsewhere, which is why, old friend I have begged you to leave Mona now, and flee, perhaps to Erin. You are too important to be lost'

Lorchar and Ceriod sat white faced and shocked at the bluntness of Owain's assessment of the situation, but the Head Druid merely smiled and ran his fingers through his long, silky white beard.

'Your assessment of the situation is just as I thought Owain, and I thank you for your honesty. But it is equally true that, to the Romans, I am too important to be let go. They will already be watching, and if they did not see me go, then Maelgwyn's minions will, and they will ensure the Romans know of it. No, I am afraid that it is my duty to remain, and to die on Mona, I will not allow them to take me in chains to Rome. We must use our warriors to kill as many of them as possible and my Druids will rain curses on them and turn their bowels to water, by making them see things they will not wish to see, but from what you tell me the average legionnaire will be more afraid of his own Centurion than anything we can throw at them.'

Owain was by now puzzled and worried by the turn of events. What did this cunning and wise old man, his dearest friend, want of him that he would not like? Surely he knew that he would fight and die to protect him, yes, and even sacrifice the life of his beloved son as well, if need be. He did not have long to wait for his answer.

'Owain my old friend, what I must ask of you is not to remain here on Mona and lead our fight against the Romans. It is true that there is no one better than you to do that, but as you have indicated the cause is futile and I have a more vital task that only you can do. I know your views about religion, and about what you are pleased to call 'magic', but I know you to be a man devoted to what we know of as the Truth in its broadest sense. To maintain it there must be Druids, and to keep the people believing in the power of Druids, some of them must be of exceptional abilities. Take it from me, there are people who can see the future, see into the minds of men, control the dreams of mighty warriors and direct the spirits of nature to good ends. I know you find this hard to believe, but if you accept my quest, you will come to see this in the months to come.'

'When we here on Mona are all destroyed there will still be many wise Druids all over Britain, but they work in isolation. Here on Mona we have a number of young novitiate Druids with huge potential but they still have a huge amount to learn to be able to control their powers for good and for the Truth. They have the future of the culture of Britain and the Truth in their hands. One of them, a young lad called Alwyn has the kind of power we only see one of in two or three generations. He could be a future Head Druid, if there ever is such a thing again. Lord Maelgwyn, who I know that you despise, has found out about him and will seek to kill him if the Romans do not. This cannot be allowed to happen. Therefore my charge to you, if you are willing to accept it, is to spirit this young protege and three other exceptional young people off this island and take them safely to two of the most sacred places I shall tell you of, where they can receive the further training they need. Also to remove two vital relics from falling into the hands of the Romans by taking them to Erin. This task is the most important thing that I can now cause to happen, and no one is better suited to the task than you. What say you Owain the Gladiator?'

Owain sat in silence for several long moments, his face white and his lips tight. Eventually he spoke, his voice shaking with emotion.

'Myrthin, you are my lord and my oldest friend. I owe you everything, my life and my freedom, the many years of happiness I have enjoyed here on Mona. I have to confess, I had thought that I would be ending my life here in your defence very soon. Now you tell me that you need me, your greatest warrior to nursemaid some children convinced they have magical powers. Why do you need me for such a task? However, before you answer, let me say this. I will do whatever you require of me Lord Myrthin. If you asked, I would walk into the flaming gates of Hades (Assuming I believed in such a place) without a moments hesitation, such is the love and respect I owe to you'

Lord Myrthin got slowly to his feet, walked over to Owain who had also risen, and embraced him.

'Thank you old friend. Your words mean much to me, and I do owe you a full explanation. Spies, those of Rome and the paid informers of Lord Maelgwyn are watching Mona closely and no large party could hope to leave the island without attracting attention. This party of young people must leave with the minimum protection that will ensure their safety without causing suspicion. Therefore, the party will consist of two young men and two young women, accompanied only by you, your son Garth and the Lady Lorchar here. The party will travel as entertainers, they have considerable skills in that direction. With you as their owner, your son as company and a woman for decencies sake, as two of the young people are girls who have reached puberty. You and Garth are more than capable of dealing with bands of robbers. Do not underestimate Lorchar's fighting ability, she is a Pictish Princess and more than able to look after herself in a fight, and she has . . . certain abilities that you may find useful. The young people too, although they are far from the finished article, have talents that you cannot even conceive of, that will be valuable in difficult situations. One of them, Branwen, who I believe you have already met?' Here Myrthin's serious face broke into a wicked smile, 'And she is the most gifted healer I have ever met with the exception of her mother, furthermore, she has a number of other accomplishments that you will find valuable on your journey. You have one week to get to know them and work on their fighting skills. By that time you must be ready to go, and to ensure that these young people survive, and have the chance to learn what they will need to ensure all we hold dear is carried on for the future. When you have got to know them better I will brief you of their other capabilities. They will be vital to your survival, so put aside your prejudices and put your faith in me and in them'

In the next house, the one owned by Lorchar, five young people reacted to being penned together with people they did not know well, for reasons that seemed mysterious and even threatening, in very different ways. It was impossible not to notice the tall athletic boy of fifteen or so with long, thick, tawny hair and curious, light, almost amber eyes who moved restlessly round the large, circular room, with scarcely hidden impatience and flickers of real anger. His movements were fast and fluid and those compelling amber eyes flashed as he muttered continually to himself. When he nearly knocked over a large pot, a girl of similar age and height but slender and with long auburn curls and pale green eyes, got up and moved to him, seizing his wrist and whispering urgently to him. At first, he just seemed angered by the intervention, but the appeal in the girl's eyes, and the soft words she spoke seemed to calm him for a while, and he went to sit back down next to her. Alwyn, who had been sitting, head in hands in a kind of reverie, lifted his head at the commotion, and then smiled across at the small scruffy girl who had been watching him intently. She grinned back in a cheerful way, and lifted up a plate of sweetened oatmeal biscuits that had been left for their refreshment, offering them to him. Alwyn took one and smiled again, as the blond giant that everyone on Mona knew was Owain's son, Garth moved with amazing rapidity for one so large and grabbed a great handful of the biscuits. He had the good grace to apologise for his greed.

'I'm sorry, but I'm starved, I thought I was eating next door with my father tonight, and I have had nothing to eat since noon' He grinned a huge good natured smile and his bright blue eyes shone in the firelight bringing return smiles from both the girls, a cheeky one from Branwen, and a shy one from the tall red headed girl. It was at this moment that Lorchar entered, and the room became silent, aware that this could be the moment that they learned why they had been brought together. The Pictish Princess-Druid hesitated for a moment then spoke.

'I am sorry that you have had to wait here in ignorance of what is happening, but events of great moment are taking shape about us, and you are all vital to what happens next. You five have been specially selected by Lord Myrthin because of your exceptional abilities. Yes, and that does include you Garth and not just because of your fighting talents. It seems likely that in the next few months the life and culture we have created here on Mona will be destroyed. There is little we can do to prevent that. But Lord Myrthin wants to think of the future of the whole island of Britain and the Truth that we as Druids are sworn to protect. You are the future of all we hold dear, and we cannot afford to lose you, and the special abilities you have now, and those you will develop with further training. Therefore, in one week you will leave Mona for the mainland under the protection of Lord Owain, Garth and myself, and for some time we will travel to two of Britain's most sacred places and stay with some of the greatest Druids not based here on Mona, with whom you will develop your skills, and use them to defend the Truth, and maintain our beliefs and our culture for future generations. Further, using those powers to remove two of our culture's most sacred relics and to keep them safe from those who would use them for ill, take them to Erin where their Druids will know how to use them for good. All of this will be dangerous, we have powerful enemies. But to stay here will be suicide and too much will be lost as it is, without losing you. You will have questions to ask'

The first to respond was Garth, his blue eyes were large with disbelief and his weather beaten face had turned white.

'My father and I have spent months preparing the warriors to repulse the Romans. Now you tell us that we are not to fight and if need be, die with them here on Mona. I cannot believe that my father has agreed to this. Instead of dying honourably with our swords in our hands, we are to nursemaid these children round Britain!'

At this point his speech was interrupted by an explosion of rage from Pered, for that was the name of the tall, restless boy. His voice was incongruously rich and resonant and his words thrummed around the room in a way that forced all to listen.

'I for one am no child and I need no nursemaid, least of all a musclebound youth barely a year older than me, Garth ap Owain, and I too had hoped to play my part in fighting off the invaders who seek to destroy our beliefs and culture. All of my years of training will be in vain if Mona and all it stands for is swept away'

Another voice broke in this point, as powerful and compelling as Pered's in its own way but gentler and persuasive rather than compelling. Melodious and lilting, it calmed the fraught atmosphere in seconds. It came from the tall red haired girl, Cerna, Pered's twin sister.

'Brother, we are not warriors, our skills are to carry our culture to others, me through my singing, you through your playing and your tales of the gods and heroes. If the Romans do come and destroy all we hold dear here in Mona, who will pass on what we know and what Alwyn here knows if we do not? We have special skills we are told, given only to one in a generation. Did the Gods give us these talents to lose them now when we still have so much more to learn? Or did they give them to us to carry them on around

Britain to enlighten people as to the Truth, and pass them on to future generations?'

Lorchar smiled at Cerna as she spoke again. 'Cerna is right, we cannot hope to defeat the Romans and unless we protect what we value in some other way, we lose all' She turned to the two young people who had not spoken yet. 'Alwyn, Branwen, both of you, for different reasons knew something of this, what do you say?'

Alwyn, pale and thoughtful raised his intelligent eyes and spoke. 'What Lorchar says is true, I have seen it in my dreams, the sort of dreams I have come to learn, that let me know of the Truth to come. All that is precious to us about Mona will be destroyed. But that does not mean that all we know and all we have learned must be lost as well. I have learned that there are others, besides the Romans who would either control us or kill us. For me there is much I still want to learn, and I want such talents as I have to be put to some use for others before I die. So, though I am filled with fear at what lies beyond the Straits, and I am sad to leave Mona at such a time of crisis, I accept that leave we must if we are to do what we as Druids and Bards are sworn to do, that is preserve the Truth. I beg you all to work together for that end'

Now it was the turn of Branwen.

'I have not the advantages some of you have had in the form of learned tutors, at least not until two years ago when my mother died, and Lord Myrthin and Lady Lorchar took me under their wings. But I was born on this island, and have never left it, all I have ever loved is here, but I know that we cannot afford to lose the talents each of us have, we must pass them on. I did not know that my talents, apart from my knowledge of medicine, were special until recently, but now I do and I know what I must do. We cannot have better protectors than Lord Owain, Garth and Lady Lorchar, but our special talents too will help us us on the journey we must take. I am the youngest, and fear what happens next, but if I accept it then surely you can as well'

Whilst she had been speaking Lord Myrthin and Owain had entered the room behind her, now they stepped forward. Beaming at Branwen, Myrthin congratulated her on her speech.

'Well said, young Branwen, I hope you are all now convinced by her eloquence. If not, here is the greatest warrior in the land, Owain the Gladiator, who has now been persuaded that his duty lies in helping to ensure your safety, as you continue your education in several places across Britain so in the future you can preserve and pass on the truth to future generations whatever happens here. Now Lord Owain wishes to speak to you.'

The grizzled old warrior squared his feet and threw back his massive shoulders before speaking.

'None of this is as we had planned and hoped, but Lord Myrthin is my oldest friend and his wisdom is beyond question. We are all of us now bound for a long and dangerous quest. On it, we will meet those who bear us no good will at all. Garth and I are expert warriors and I am told that the Lady Lorchar is skilled with weapons as well. The rest of you are very young, and your training, though extensive, has not, I think, covered the fighting arts. In one week I must try to ensure that all of you can at least look after yourself in a fight. I am told that all of you have talents beyond the range of the rest of us that will be useful on our journey, and against our enemies. I warn you I am sceptical of anything that smacks of 'Magic', but it would be useful at this stage to know what these talents are'

It was, to Owain's surprise, Myrthin himself who spoke up.

'Very well Owain. It is well that all should know what each can offer. Let me begin with young Alwyn. He is what we know as a 'Seer' In his dreams he can see much of what is to happen. Furthermore he has the power when required to see into men's minds and he is just beginning to learn how to put thoughts into the minds of others. No one will be able to entirely take you by surprise whilst you have Alwyn in your midst. However, you must all be careful, as the gift of seeing into the future is a capricious one, often you will learn what might happen if you do or do not do certain things, so beware of relying upon it. The twins Pered and Cerna are Bards, Their playing, singing and story telling will make you welcome anywhere. But their talents go further than this.

Cerna's singing has the power to instantly change the emotions of her listeners. Normally she fills them with joy but equally she can stir them to righteous anger or fill them with abject fear. With further training she will be able to sing people the song of their lives and when she has done that no one will harm her.

Her brother Pered is an able Harpist but his true talent lies in his voice and his memory. I have never known anyone able to memorise the stories of the people of Britain and their Gods as quickly as him and when he tells the stories he holds his audience literally spellbound. His voice has other properties as well and with training no one will be able to resist his commands, especially when he has learned the Words of Power.

The twins have lived here for several years but they come originally from King Maelor's lands in the South West, so they will be pleased to return there if only for a while.

Young Branwen you already know something of. She is a truly gifted healer, trained by her mother, the best there was. She was raised in the forest and is what we Druids call 'treewise', which means that she is part of the forest herself and whether you believe it or not, she can call on the spirits and creatures of the forest in ways you will find useful. In addition she has the ability to disappear at will. This is something even I do not understand fully, but I am sure you will find it valuable, if frustrating when she has chores to complete.' at this he looked at Branwen with great fondness and she grinned back at him.

'I will leave the Lady Lorchar to explain her special talents to you herself but perhaps at a time when you might be a little more open to believing her than you are at present'

There was silence for a moment and much looking around at the faces of the young people whose skills had been so briefly summarized. Then Owain spoke again

'Very well, I will look forward to seeing those talents for myself. In the meantime I still need to assess your skills with weapons and give you what training we can in the short time available. Go to your beds now, and try to get some sleep. In the morning, at first light, I expect to see you on the hill above the village where the warriors usually train. Dress appropriately and ensure you are well fed, for tomorrow will be long and hard.' With these words he and Garth left and Myrthin and Lorchar moved round the group of bemused young students giving each words of reassurance and encouragement before they attempted to switch off the thoughts and fears that flashed round their minds and seize an hour or two of sleep.

At first light the next morning, a cool haze rose from the still dewy grass, but a blue sky promised another fine, warm day to come. Owain stood like a statue, oblivious to the cool air in the short Roman tunic he preferred to train in, whilst Garth, dressed in check trousers and a sleeveless leather jerkin that displayed his muscular ams, laid out a selection of real and training weapons on blankets on the short, damp grass. Owain was watching the group he now had to assess and train as they walked up the hill towards him. He could see he would not have to worry about Lorchar. She moved up the steep hill with rapid purpose and she wore a fighting outfit of tight, soft leather that did not hide her lean muscular body. Over her shoulder was a hunting bow and a quiver of arrows. On her belt was a short, slim sword and several daggers. This was a woman used to war, and in her fighting prime still. Owain nodded to himself in approval. Branwen ran at Lorchar's heels, dressed in green trousers and shirt, and equipped with a bow and arrows and two long, wickedly sharp daggers. She was small, but Owain judged that she was fit and used to the outdoors and she gave off an air of one who could look after herself. The twins and Alwyn walked together. Pered was tall and strong looking and had a look of fierce determination on his face as he strode up the hill. Owain decided that if he could keep this young man calm enough, he could turn him into a warrior. The other two gave him concern. Cerna just seemed too gentle to be a fighter, and Alwyn with his slender build and faraway look, just did not have warrior stamped upon him. Still, Owain would have to ensure they had the basic skills needed to defend themselves in a fight. Much as he respected Myrthin, he could not bring himself to believe that the 'special' skills the old Druid had described the previous night would be any value in the hurly burly of an attack. When all were gathered before him, Owain spoke to them.

'Friends, we have much to do today and I ask you not to be offended by anything I say to you. All will be to help you reach a level where I can be confident that in a fight, I do not have to watch your backs as well as my own. First I need to assess your present skill and potential. Lady Lorchar, normally, your seniority would mean I would begin with you, but on this, I trust Lord Myrthin's opinion and the evidence of my own eyes. You do not have to prove anything.' Lorchar smiled quickly, but her face was set, her eyes determined.

'I thank you Owain, but from now on, we are one team and everyone must have confidence in each other. First, everyone from now on must call me Lorchar, the title does not matter. Secondly, whatever tests you have prepared for the others, I too will undergo.' Owain nodded his approval

'Very well Lorchar, the first test is single combat. Pick a training weapon that suits you and you shall compete with Garth for a few minutes. Lorchar picked out a short sword and a dagger from the pile of blunted weapons used for training, and dropped her bow, quiver and sword belt on the grass. Garth picked up a long sword and and a round buckler and took up a fighting stance in front of Lorchar, whose own stance, Owain noted with approval, was no less professional than his son's. On a nod from the old gladiator the two circled each other cautiously, before Garth essayed an exploratory jab with his long sword. Quickly, and with some expertise Lorchar used her sword and dagger to force up Garth's blade and aim a sharp kick at his groin. Garth jumped back and used his great power to bring down a rain of powerful blows at his opponent. Lorchar skillfully parried these blows, but was having to give ground quickly and as she tried a jab of her own, lost her balance and found Garth's sword at her throat.

Owain was more than pleased with Lorchar's performance and told her so, reminding the Pictish princess that hardly a warrior in Britain would have done better against Garth's skill, strength and speed. Lorchar did not seem pleased with the compliment however and replied with some asperity.

'He needs to finish the job more quickly, in real combat this would have been the result' With these words, a small dagger appeared in her hand and with a rapid underhand flick it stuck, quivering in a nearby tree.

'Even more impressive Lorchar, I do not envy a warrior that dares to underestimate your fighting skill.' said Owain with a pacifying laugh as he helped Lorchar to her feet and then studied the beautifully balanced dagger Garth had pulled from the tree.

'Specially made for me by a skilled armourer' said Lorchar 'I aways have several about me and I am deadly accurate up to about twenty feet'

Owain turned to the others. 'I do not expect any of you to be as skilled as Lorchar with weapons, I am looking at your potential Pered. You are tall and well set up, let us see what you can do'

Pered nodded briefly and moved to the pile of training weapons. Owain and Garth noted with approval that he discarded several, before finding a long, slim, well balanced sword and a light shield. When Garth took up his stance, the other boy simply flew at him with astonishing speed and ferocity. Pered had no finesse, but the sheer speed of his attack drove Garth backwards for a few seconds. Garth retained his composure, parried Pered's rapid jabs and slashes and, as the other boy began to tire, feinted a high slash at the head of his opponent and at the last moment, changed it into a cut at the legs which knocked Pered off his feet. Again Owain congratulated the loser.

'Well done young man, you gave Garth quite a shock with your speed and ferocity. What we need to do, is to teach you some defensive skills and try to instill a cooler head when you are in combat. Though I have to say, not many experienced warriors could have stood up to that onslaught'

These words and the evident sincerity of Owain's compliment seemed to take the heat out of the fury in Pered's eyes and the tension in his mouth faded into a half smile as he replied.

'Thank you sir, from you the those words mean a great deal. Believe me I am a quick learner and I will not be fooled by such a ploy again' then the smile faded again and the lad directed a look of real fury at Garth, who merely smiled and shrugged.

Owain now turned to Branwen, 'Young lady you are as yet very small and slight and it would seem futile to set you against Garth . . .' He did not have time to finish his words as Branwen interjected with furious anger.

'I may be small in size, but I have lived wild in the forest by myself for months at a time. In combat I have skills you cannot dream of and I have no fear of any big ox of a warrior—no insult intended Garth!'

Owain bellowed out a great laugh at the fury of this tiny young girl.

'Very well young woman, let us see what you can do, choose your weapons.'

Casting aside her bow and arrows and dagger belt, she selected two training daggers as she stood to face an opponent half as tall again as her, and three times her weight. Garth advanced towards her with a grin on his face, in stark contrast to the fierce intensity of Branwen's face. Just at that moment there came the loud call of a red deer stag in the copse behind them, and all faces turned briefly towards the noise. Garth turned back and his fierce little opponent had simply disappeared. He rushed forward to see if she was hidden in some long grass, and all there on the hillside, except Lorchar had shocked looks on their faces. At that moment, as if from nowhere, Branwen, reappeared, flat on the ground behind Garth's feet, which were instantly pulled away from him and he fell flat on his face on the ground, whereupon Branwen leapt on his back and seized his long hair, dragging his head back and in the same move passing the blunt dagger across his throat.

'Size and strength' she said in an amused voice 'Are useful, but they are not the only asset in a fight!' There ensued general uproar as Garth protested that magic had been used, Owain denied that there was any such thing as magic and Alwyn, Pered and Cerna just laughed uproariously. Lorchar just stood and smiled for a few moments before taking charge of the situation.

'I had not intended that any of the special talents of the young people would be displayed today, but Branwen is something of a free spirit, and perhaps it is no bad thing for you prosaic warriors to see that there is more to this little group than a collection of vulnerable students. I have seen Branwen do this little disappearing act several times and must confess that neither Myrthin or I know how it is done. Strangely enough, neither does Branwen herself, she merely says that when she needs to disappear she does. She can still see all that is happening and can reappear at will.'

Owain shook his head 'I was going to say that I had never seen such a thing in my life, but of course I have, is that not so Branwen, because that is how you, er, caught me unawares the other day, yes? But tell me, that sound of a stag that distracted Garth, your doing, or a mere coincidence?' Branwen, delighted at the attention thrown her way by the feat, grinned brightly before replying.

'I knew the stag was there, because, well, I just always do know such things, and I was able to call on it to cry out by just thinking it, and then use the distraction to disappear. As Lorchar says I do not know how I do that. I have been able to do it since I was a child and it used to drive my mother to distraction' At the mention of her mother, the cheeky grin faded from her face and a small tear appeared at the corner of her eye.

Owain and Lorchar exchanged a look, as they were both reminded that despite her talents, and her defiant attitude, they were dealing with a young girl to whom a great deal had happened in quite a short time, and she would need careful handling. Owain decided to move on with the assessment.

'Well Garth if you have recovered from the shock of what just happened, perhaps we should give Alwyn a try?'

The pale young man with the intense, intelligent blue eyes glanced across at Owain and with a shrug stepped forward and picked up a slim, mid length sword well suited to his light build. Garth stepped up to face him and looked quizzically at the lad. 'No shield, Alwyn?'

The young Druid smiled quickly.'No Garth, this is enough for me to handle, I am unused to these exertions'

The two young men faced each other and Garth seemed a little unnerved by the intensity of the gaze that Alwyn directed at him, but he shrugged and aimed a powerful jab at Alwyn's chest. It was immediately parried by Alwyn and Garth essayed a powerful downward chop at his opponent' s head and shoulders. Alwyn again parried the blow, though he staggered a little at the power of it. Garth, by now a little irritated, unleashed a whirlwind of jabs, cuts and feints but Alwyn was always prepared for the shot. He was forced backwards by Garth's strength, and the blows were clearly taking their toll on his stamina, but he always seemed able to second guess what the next attack would be, as Garth tried out all the tricks his father had taught him. However, it seemed that soon, Garth must wear out his slighter built, untrained opponent, when suddenly Garth gave a yell and hurled his sword aside with a look of pure horror. With a quick smile

Alwyn stepped forward and put his sword to Garth's throat. Owain gasped in disbelief

'How did you do that Alwyn? You have little stamina or strength, and no training in combat, yet you correctly anticipated each move of my son, who is one of the most skillful sword fighters in Britain. And what caused Garth to hurl his weapon away like that? Another trick?'

Alwyn looked cooly back at the great warrior.

'No 'trick' sir, merely a different kind of skill. No doubt, in combat you are able, through your experience and skill to tell what an opponent can do. Well, in certain circumstances, I am able to do the same by simply reading his thoughts, I can anticipate his next move. However, he is so much stronger than I am, and he would soon have defeated me by pure strength, and my own lack of combat fitness. I thought it would be useful to show you that, though I am not born to be a warrior, I have other talents that may be valuable. The other day Garth told me he had a particular horror of adders, I merely put into his head the thought that he was not holding a sword, but a serpent. The result you saw.'

Owain shook his head in astonishment,' I have to tell you all, that what I have seen here this morning has shaken me to my core. All my beliefs, I must now hold up to question, for today I have seen skills and talents that I simply cannot comprehend. However, now I do understand why my old friend Myrthin thought your lives were worth taking special care to preserve. So young lady Cerna, have you anything to show us that will also amaze and astonish this old warrior?'

The tall, slender girl stood up and smiled uncertainly at Owain, 'I hope so sir. I certainly have no skill at combat, though I know how to use my bow. Most of my life so far has been devoted to music, though recently I have been shown that my voice has certain properties that may be useful to us in our dangerous quest.'

Even in her speaking voice, her listeners found themselves feeling calmer and less agitated by the morning's marvels. As the girl walked gracefully over to the pile of training weapons, she began singing softly and sadly. She picked up a short sword, and turned to face Garth, and began singing more loudly and more directly at the young warrior. Garth seemed utterly transfixed, and as the singing continued, his eyes filled with tears and soon he was sobbing uncontrollably. Cerna slowly walked up to him and removed the great sword from his hand, and still singing, embraced the sobbing youth, comforting him in his grief. Owain spluttered out a question.

'How on earth did you do that Cerna? I mean, I felt the sadness in your song, but not to the extent that I would have been unable to fight?' Cerna smiled,

'It was intended only for Garth. Lorchar tells me that, in time, I will be able to do this to a whole audience, but for the time being, I can only reach that level of intensity on one person. I sang to Garth of loss, having sensed that he has experienced loss in his life. Garth, I am sorry if it it has upset you greatly, but I felt it was important that I showed, that despite my lack of talent for combat, I could use those abilities I do possess in a way that will be helpful in our quest. Do you forgive me?' As she said this she tenderly wiped the tears from Garth's cheek, only adding to his confusion.

'Cerna, of course it was a strange experience for me, being overwhelmed by emotion in a combat situation, I felt so struck with loss, that I could do nothing but think of my poor mother. But I have seen such marvels today, that in fact. I now feel more confident about our mission than I did a few hours ago. Thank you too, for your kindness. I am recovered now.'

Owain spoke up again. 'Very well, Garth and I have been taught some lessons today that show us that strength, skill and speed in fighting are not the only useful attributes we will have available to us in our long and dangerous travels. However, Lord Myrthin himself believes that those skills that Garth and I have will be essential, so perhaps we should show you what we can do. Believe me, in the months to come there will be times when your special Druidical talents will be difficult to use effectively, and you will need simple fighting skills. Garth, do you feel ready to show what we can do'

Garth nodded and picked up the long, heavy training sword again, along with a shield, while Owain chose a blunted version of his own favourite Roman gladius and the small buckler shield he favoured.

The powerful old warrior and his tall, athletic son faced each other for a moment, and then leaped together in a rapid clash of iron. The conflict was going to hinge on whether Owain's immense strength and years of experience, was going to be enough to overcome Garth's speed and unforgiving stamina. Garth's long sword swung in great arcs, or jabbed forward in seemingly unavoidable thrusts, but Owain parried each and every one with sword or shield and then counterattacked with mighty blows of his own. Owain needed to get in close to use his strength, and his shorter stabbing sword. Garth did his best to keep his distance, and use the longer reach and slashing capacity of his British sword. Owain's strength was still terrifying, but he no longer had the speed or stamina of his youth, and the longer the combat went on, the more it seemed that Owain must tire and his son prevail.

Owain in his experience, knew this only too well and risked all on a move that would either win him a victory, or cause his son to win the day, if it failed. He sidestepped a thrust from Garth, ducked down, and moved in with his shield in a furious upward push. He caught the younger man under the ribs, and continued to follow through, lifting the young giant clean off his feet and on to his back where in a split second, Garth felt the blunted point of his father's sword against his throat. Garth banged the ground in frustration.

'I almost had you there father, another minute and you would have been too exhausted to continue, I must learn more patience.' Owain's barrel chest rose and fell rapidly as Owain gasped for breath and wiped the sweat from his eyes.

'Indeed you must son. That was the closest yet! Very soon now I must face the fact that that my young son can defeat me in combat' He turned to the others 'Though I tell you all that I still believe that he will be the only man in Britain who can, and I am the only Briton or Roman who can defeat Garth'

Over the next few days the seven worked long hours, with the three experienced warriors training the four younger ones how to use the weapons effectively. They practiced with their bows until they were hitting moving targets. They fought each other to exhaustion, and the two adults knew that the younger people were improving their fitness for the ordeals of travelling for months on end. Sometimes Myrthin came to watch. He approved of the progress the youngsters were making, but all the same he often looked very sad. One day he spoke of his feelings to Owain.

'Rest tomorrow, my friend, for tomorrow night you must all leave the island. I will never again see some of the people I care most about in the whole world. You are my oldest and dearest friend. I have watched you change from that wild and angry ex gladiator, that accompanied me back to Mona from Rome twenty years ago, to a kind and thoughtful leader of men. I will miss you and your fine son more than I can say. What I kept from you is that Lorchar has been my lover and friend these past seven years, you can trust her with your life. You can guess what I feel about losing her, and it was not easy to get her to leave. Only her loyalty to me, and her belief in our cause, persuaded her to go. You may have noticed the fondness with which I regard young Branwen. Before Lorchar, Branwen's mother was my lover, and in fact, the girl is my daughter, my only child. She does not know this, she regards me as a fond uncle, she does not know how desperate I was when her mother died and Branwen went missing in the forest. I had always intended to tell her the truth one day, and make her a Druid, she has abilities you cannot begin to imagine. However, now, the day of our parting is not the time to tell her. I trust you and Lorchar to tell her when the time feels right, after I am dead' At this, tears filled the old Druid's eyes and he was for a moment overcome with emotion, but he gathered in his feelings and continued. 'As for the other three, their talents and characters make them almost unique in their generation and I had hoped to play a longer role in their training and development, especially Alwyn, who I see as a future Head Druid. Now others must finish the task, and I charge you, Owain, to do your utmost to protect them from harm, for as long as you are able.' Owain seized Myrthin's wrist in his massive hand, causing the older man to wince with pain.

'Myrthin, I owe you the happiness I have enjoyed these twenty years. It was you that won me my freedom and brought me back here to the green land that I love. You, who introduced me to my dear wife, and bought me back from black depression when she died, and gave me new purpose in bringing up my boy to the fine young man he is now. You know that I care little for religion, but I know that you have always fought for what is right and decent and that is religion enough for me. You tell me that these young people are special, to the future of our people, and your word will suffice. Now you tell me how much some of us mean to you, that you will see them go, knowing you will never see us again. My old friend, I will defend them with my last drop of blood, and will do all in my power to see that what you will for us is accomplished—this is my oath. I will swear by no Gods but by the bonds of our friendship.'

In the fading light the warrior and the Druid walked down the hill arm in arm, and in silent thought.

Chapter 4

The following evening, a small party well laden with baggage made their way to a small secluded bay on the east coast of Mona. Owain was dressed in British clothes of checked wool and like the others he wore a warm cloak against the evening chill. In his right hand he carried a massive oak staff, iron shod at both ends. In his belt he carried a gladius and Roman dagger, on his shoulder he carried his shield. Garth had a huge axe as well as a shield on his shoulders, and in his belt his favourite long sword. Lorchar, dressed all over in leather had a bow and a quiver of arrows and belt studded with throwing daggers. Branwen was similarly armed and was dressed in warm wool in her favourite forest green. Alwyn had a small harp in a leather pouch across his back and wore a slender sword at his waist. Pered carried a similar harp, but carried a boar spear as a staff, and wore a long sword and dagger at his belt and what he fondly believed was a belligerent warrior's glare on his young face. Cerna was the only one of the females in the party to wear a skirt, kirtled up for travelling, with long boots of soft leather on her feet. She too, carried a bow and arrows, but no sword, just a long slender dagger. They rode on ponies, with further ponies carrying bundles of clothes and some food for the journey. As they rode down the long narrow valley to the beach, they saw a boat and some men gathered around it. Talking to the four boatmen was Lord Myrthin himself. For the first time since Owain had known him Myrthin looked anxious and upset. He drew Owain aside and spoke quietly and urgently to his old friend.

'Owain, it seems to me most likely that I will never see any of you again. It may be futile, but when the Romans come, we intend to fight them to the death. None of us here have any desire to be dragged off to Rome as slaves, for the edification of the crowds. On a personal level, tonight I am saying goodbye to one of my oldest and most loyal friends and his son, a fine young man who I have become very fond of; my lover, the finest and bravest of women; my daughter, who I love dearly, though for her sake I have never acknowledged our relationship, and three fine young people who I had hoped to see develop into the future of the Druids and Bards of Britain. Beyond that, the mission you begin tonight, with no guarantee of success, is only happening because soon, that which Mona stands for, learning, peace and the Truth, that which it has provided for the island of Britain and for all the people who share our culture across the world for hundreds of years, could soon all be destroyed.'

'These young people, under the protection of you and Lorchar, are the only hope that what we believe in here on Mona will survive in future generations. You know you will face many dangers. Not only greedy and uncaring fools and brigands on the road, but powerful and evil enemies who actively wish you harm. Maelgwyn, with his many powers and his loyal supporters, can not be easily set aside, and what he knows, eventually the Romans will know too. They hate us, and wish to see us destroyed, and I have reasons, which I cannot disclose, to believe, that before this year is out they will have even greater reason to hate all that Druids stand for. Once they have rumours of you and your mission, they too will seek you out and try to kill or capture you all. Tonight, you will be taken to a secret landing place deep in the Conwy valley. From there, avoiding territory controlled by Maelgwyn you must travel south and west to where the land of the Demetae meets the Hibernian Sea, The Druid you must meet there will make contact with Alwyn in ways known only to the adept. In the same way Alwyn will know that he bears you no evil. He will help Alwyn, and maybe some of the others, for as long as he dares, before sending you on to your next destination. He will also give you Aneurin's Torc for safe keeping. It must not fall into the hands of Maelgwyn or the Romans, for they would use its power for ill ends. From there you must go to Ynys Avalon and meet with Eirlys the White Druid of Avalon, she is very wise and will advise you further and will pass into your safe keeping the Cauldron of the Kings of Erin. Then these two precious objects must be taken to Erin. The Druids there will know of your coming and the return of the Cauldron after hundreds of years in our possession will mean that you receive a warm welcome. No doubt you will need to stay there a while, the young people will have much to assimilate by this time and maybe some sad news from Mona to come to terms with.' Here Myrthin stopped for a while, seeming to need a moment to master his feelings. Owain squeezed his shoulder with as much gentleness as he was capable of and smiled though his own thoughts were in a spin at what this remark heralded. Myrthin took a deep breath, and with his voice cracking with emotion, continued speaking. 'For the forseeable future yours will be an uncertain and dangerous life, and I know you do not share all my beliefs. The fact that you are still prepared to do it, risking your life and that of your son, out of loyalty to me, and your own half formed belief in what we call the Truth, touches me more than I can say. Do not say anything now old friend, it has been hard enough for me to keep my feelings in check already, and I must say my farewells to the others now. Goodbye Owain, I know that our Gods and spirits will be with you on your journey, whether you believe in them or not. I believe your destiny will be to repay me for what little I was able to do for you, with a task which will make you and Lorchar and these young people the subject of songs and tales for hundreds of years to come.'

With these words Myrthin embraced Owain, leaving both of them close to tears before he turned to the others and spoke with a catch in his normally resonant voice.

'Now you must begin your quest. Four of you, to gain knowledge and understanding of the rare powers and talents you possess. In part, you will be guided and protected by the other three. But the powers you will learn to use will enable you to look after the wellbeing of the whole group, and as a recognition of your unique qualities, I now pronounce that the four of you, despite your youth, and in one case lack of formal education, are full Druids with all the power and honour due to that rank and all the protection afforded by those that serve the Truth!' Whilst the four young Druids took a moment to take in the huge honour that had been awarded to them, Myrthin spoke briefly to the others. 'I am mindful of the sacrifices you three are making, partly out of love and respect for me and also because you recognise the importance of this quest for our culture, and for the knowledge of the Truth in the Island of Britain and elsewhere. My sacrifice is also great because I will miss your love, advice and friendship. Our people will always be grateful to you as long as this tale is told.'

He moved on to say a few words to each of the young people and Lorchar embracing each of them as he gave them his blessing along with the sad farewell. All were in tears, with Branwen and the normally icy Lorchar clearly the most upset. By now the boatmen were busying themselves loading the possessions on the boat, and fretting loudly about the tide, so the seven intrepid travellers climbed into the boat and waved final farewells to Myrthin as the boat pulled away.

As the boat sailed away, all on board looked longingly back at the coast of Mona, they saw the low green hills, the famous oak groves and the fields of oats and barley that fed so many. They looked across the narrow Straits to the mainland, with its steep mountains, shrouded as usual with menacing clouds. Each of them was wondering whether they would ever see Mona's gently rolling hills again. At that moment the clouds rolled away for a brief few moments, and silver moonlight, washed over the land and lit the sea between the boat and the island, giving the whole scene a magical glow which brought tears back to the eyes of several of the inhabitants of the boat.

A few hours later, before the dawn stole over the mainland, and after a mercifully calm crossing, the small boat crept for several miles up the river Conwy until a dim light moving back and fore on the eastern shore of the river signalled they were at their prepared landing place, a narrow river beach overhung with tall trees. There, a small group of men waited with ten ponies, packed up with food, drink and clothes for the ongoing journey. Very few words were said, and the shivering men on the riverbank clearly held the two powerful warriors and the five Druids in considerable awe.

Soon the party of seven on their long quest, led the ponies away from the well marked track at the bottom of the valley, up through the trees, to a narrower, darker path through the forest that clothed the hillside. Owain briefly told the others that they had better push on for a few hours away from the well populated area near the river estuary, before they dare stop for a rest and some food. So, in silent, single file the group moved south through the dense forest. Owain took the lead position and Garth took the rearmost spot. In between the others were left to their thoughts. Lorchar rode head down, clearly still sad at the finality of her goodbyes with Myrthin. Behind her, Alwyn looked around thoughtfully, but often seemed to drift into a kind of reverie, allowing his pony to pick its own way along the path. Next came Cerna, humming happily to herself as she seemed to be composing a new song of their adventures. Her brother was directly behind her, his eyes darting around at the slightest forest sound, seemingly almost wishing for some danger to arise so that he could rush to meet it.

Of all of the party only Branwen was now on foot, indeed, she had now hung her shoes over her saddle and was skipping barefoot along the forest path. Her eyes were shining with a kind of greenish light. It was in the forest, any forest that Branwen felt most at home. She could hear, and identify any noise in the forest, down to the tiniest shrew moving swiftly through the leaf litter. All the trees and plants were old friends to her, and she knew all their uses, but most of all, the spirits of the forest spoke to her as though they recognised her as kin. Her very soul sang in the forest, and where others might fear, she was in her element, and no creature or plant held any fears for her. She experienced a kind of tingling through her skin, and the blood in her veins coursed more strongly here. To trot alongside the horses at a pace that would have tired most, was no effort to her, and the tiredness she had felt aboard the boat was gone, replaced with an enhanced vitality that made her feel invincible. Garth, travelling at the rear, saw this transformation, and wondered at it, but felt that, sometime in this journey, they would surely need Branwen's clear affinity with the forest and would be glad of whatever powers she could draw from it.

After a couple of hours, Owain called a halt and rather stiffly dismounted from his sturdy pony at a small glade in the forest.

'We will rest here a while and eat, the ponies at least should be given time to recover'. Branwen trotted up to him and placed her small hand on his powerful arm, quietly she spoke to the old warrior.

'Owain, I saw that your hip has some stiffness after riding, if we are lighting a fire here, allow me to prepare you an infusion that would help, I have seen some herbs here in the forest that would work with the willow bark to ease the ache, and give you energy for this afternoon's travel'

Owain smiled, and tenderly placed his hand on the girl's small head

'Bless you my dear, I can see that we will gain much from your love of the wild wood as well as your knowledge of healing. Collect your herbs, whilst we light a small fire and prepare something to eat, for we are all a little weak for lack of food today, all except you I expect'

Whilst the others set about collecting dry wood for a fire and settling the ponies, Branwen disappeared off into the forest. As soon as she was away from the others Branwen discarded all her clothes, and ran naked through the forest, barely seeming to touch the forest floor. She came to a glade, in which she seemed to know that she would find the herbs she sought, and she set about collecting them. She heard the slightest of noises in the surrounding trees, and she froze, seeming to disappear into the undergrowth. Out of the woods came a roedeer buck, which stood still in the middle of the glade as Branwen slowly approached him. The girl stretched out her hand and laid it on the neck of the deer who stood, still as a statue, whilst the girl reached down and felt the right foreleg of the buck just above its hoof. She could feel the heat of some inflammation there and as she held the leg for a few moments she could feel the heat of the sore leg move into her hand and dissipate. A long blackthorn was caught underneath the skin of the buck's leg, and Branwen's strong nails moved it along to a point at which she could extract it from the skin. She gave the leg a brief rub and laid it down. The buck looked at Branwen then moved slowly away. Even in

Branwen's early life in the forest of Mona such a thing had never happened before, though she knew she had an affinity with all of the creatures of the forest. The girl knew that something strange and significant had happened, and she could not wait to relate it to Lorchar, to see if the wise Druid could interpret the event for her. Gathering her herbs she ran back to the edge of the glade where the others were preparing food. Standing perfectly still at the edge of the glade, her tanned skin took on other shades in the tree shaded sunlight, hints of green and brown moved over her gently, the leaves of the undergrowth seemed to move closer and break up her outline and although she was only feet away from the others she was entirely invisible to them. Even Owain's combat trained eyes and Pered's sharp, ever restless eyes could not pick her up. Branwen derived a sly pleasure from knowing that she had this unique skill, and smiled quietly to herself before moving silently away, dressing quickly, and returning to the others. Branwen swiftly made up the infusion she had promised Owain and even made it pleasant to drink with the addition of some honey.

Well rested, the party soon set off again and Branwen took the opportunity of a widening of the path to move up to Lorchar and tell her quietly of the incident in the woods. The Druid smiled one of her long, thoughtful smiles and looked at Branwen with a new respect.

'You know, Branwen my dear, the spirit of the forest that some call Cerunnos, can take many forms. It is known that one he especially favours is the Roedeer buck. So I believe, young lady, that the deer you met in the forest today was no ordinary deer, but the spirit of the forest himself. We have always known that you had a special affinity for the forest and the spirits of nature, but I believe that today marks a new stage in that affinity. Cerunnos himself has shown you favour, and I believe his showing himself to you today shows that he, and maybe the gods and spirits in general, favour our quest. However, some of our number are sceptical of such manifestations and I would not want them to think less of you so it would be well if we kept this to ourselves for now. Oh! and one other thing, your skill of invisibility is very rare and will be valuable to us in our quest, but you should know that though you are invisible to normal sight you are not invisible to those of us blessed with another sort of sight. My skill in these matters is limited, but I was aware of your presence and your exact position earlier on. There are others with far greater powers who can see far more, so be warned'

Lorchar smiled at her talented protege but the girl coloured slightly at the realisation that Lorchar's words implied that Alwyn, whose quiet ways she rather liked, could well have seen her, standing there a few feet away from him, naked as a baby. The group travelled on along the wooded hills all afternoon, riding and walking to rest their horses. As evening approached, Owain called a halt.

'There is a village in the valley ahead and maybe it is time for us begin doing what we are supposed to do. That is, we approach, ask to see the village headman or chief and find out whether they would like an evening of music, song and stories in return for a meal and and somewhere warm to sleep. Are you ready for this deception and the performance you must put on?'. Most of the party agreed with alacrity, but Alwyn closed his eyes and concentrated for a few moments before speaking up.

'I sense no evil from the village so I am happy to go along with the plan. I will keep my wits about about me during the evening and night in case there is any change'

Owain and Lorchar exchanged glances of approval, before they chose a path that led down the hill to a neatly kept village of about fifteen round houses, clustered in the middle of well tended fields. As they approached the edge of the village, some young men, seeing an approaching group, with some clearly armed, picked up spears and axes, and stood in the entrance way to the village. The group stopped, and Owain walked slowly forward with his hands open in the gesture that indicated peaceful intent throughout Britain. As he did so, a powerfully built older man of about forty, with a long, untidy beard bustled forward, buckling on a sword belt as he did, with a woman just behind, holding out a shield for him. Owain stopped, and with a broad smile on his face introduced himself and his companions telling the villagers that they were a party of entertainers travelling around the west of Britain and that for a hot meal and somewhere to sleep, they would be glad to provide the village with an evening's entertainment. The man with sword stepped forward and spoke in a confident voice.

'Welcome strangers, I am Erwin, clan chief in this valley. We are always glad to hear songs and stories as well as news from elsewhere, these days, with talk of the Romans arriving in our area, we see all too few visitors. You will excuse our seemingly aggressive welcome at first, but you Master Owain, and the young man you introduced as your son, carry yourselves like warriors and you are certainly well armed'

Owain smiled again,

'You are perceptive Lord Erwin, for most of my life I have been a warrior, selling my sword arm to whoever could promise me the most gold and glory. My son too, has trained as a warrior, but the world is changing, and in a Britain more closely controlled by the Romans, we believe that this will be a more profitable way to earn our keep. So if you wish, tonight, as well as music, songs and the old tales performed by my young friends here, I will regale your company with a few stories of old battles and travels and Garth here, would be happy to wrestle with such of your young men who feel inclined to challenge him!'

The faces of the young men who stood behind Erwin brightened at this prospect and even Erwin's craggy face broke into a broad smile.

'Come then, and welcome. We will give you time to refresh yourself and a good hot meal in my house before we gather the whole village together to enjoy your entertainments!'

Erwin's roundhouse was more than twice the size of any other house in the village. Inside it was warm and comfortable, with a blazing fire, and festooned with padded furs to sit on. Erwin's wife and servants bustled round with drinks and warm oat bannocks with honey as the tired travellers took a well earned rest, many of them sleeping, whilst Erwin and Owain talked earnestly with each other for some time, each trying to learn what was new, especially about the Romans. Owain was relieved to know that no Romans had been seen in the area as yet, but concerned that news of them was coming from a few days further to the South and East. The veteran of many battles knew just how quickly the legions could move when required. Erwin was very concerned to learn that the threat to Mona was real and urgent, and promised to send word swiftly to the island when the Romans drew nearer.

After an excellent meal and some ale, the time for the evening's entertainment had arrived. Outside in the open area in the centre of the village a huge fire warmed the cooling air and an excited babble came from the the entire village who sat on the ground around the fire. Cerna, as serene and beautiful as ever stepped forward to take a central spot, flanked by Pered and Alwyn with their harps. Lorchar sat cross legged nearby with a small drum.

Pered began to play, and sighs and mutters of appreciation came from the admiring crowd as the ethereal tones of a good harp, expertly played, soared into the evening sky. Alwyn and Lorchar joined in supporting Pered's soaring melody with an exciting rhythm. Then, suddenly without warning, the first clear notes of Cerna's stunning voice came through, bringing gasps of amazement from the whole watching village. Cerna was a true artist, and for almost an hour she played the whole audience expertly. She wound them up with exciting, fast tempo songs of old heroes and then brought them to tears with unbearably sad and tragic love songs. She brought tears of laughter to them as well when she sang familiar comic songs, and got them all to sing along with time honoured favourites. Of course, it was not just her singing virtuosity that accomplished her total conquest of her audience, but her rare power of being able to read the emotions of all the people present. The village had never seen a performance like it and whistled and stamped and yelled their appreciation when she had finished.

After a short break Pered returned, this time without his harp and began to tell tales, familiar old ones at first, of the great heroes of old, of Lleu Llaw Gyfaes and his exploits. Tales of magic, the gods, of love and battle fell from his mouth and the crowd were spellbound. For a young man his voice had immense power, and his control of it was astonishing. One moment it would seem to be no more than a whisper and it would rise suddenly to a shattering scream, making even grizzled old warriors jump and spill from their alepots. Pered, like his sister, held them in the palm of his hand, until all too soon, his time was done, and as it was now late, the young children were dragged unwillingly to bed.

Owain stood and shouted out that he and Garth would complete the evening with a display of combat skills, and would take challenges from any warriors present. Father and son stripped to the waist and despite the cool evening air they were soon sweating in the firelight as they showed off their skills with a variety of weapons. One or two of the young warriors, stirred up by friends and by the presence of girls, shouted out challenges to Garth, who accepted them all with a smile and with strength and skill easily defeated the best that that the village could offer and soon his powerful physique, glistening now with the exertion attracted admiring glances and amused comments from the young women present. Erwin, sensing a growing undercurrent from the village's young bucks, jumped to his feet and throwing off his cloak and shirt, bellowed out a challenge to Owain.

'Master Owain, why should only the young warriors have all the fun. We older ones can show the youngsters a trick or two. What say we have a wrestling match, the two of us, to end tonight's entertainment?'

Owain too, had picked up on the envious mutters of some of the young men, and seized eagerly on Erwin's challenge, though truth to be told, he had stiffened up a little from his earlier exertions. The two old warriors gave a good account of themselves, making use of cunning tricks and long practiced moves to throw the other off balance. Of course Owain was the far more experienced warrior, and he quickly realised, much stronger than his wily opponent. Owain, however knew what the evening required, and at one point he was gripping his opponent in preparation for a throw, when he felt Erwin throw a leg behind him and alter his balance for a trip throw. Owain grinned briefly, and allowed the move to take its course and ended up flat on his back on the hard earth, to a huge shout of joy from the watching villagers. Erwin, laughing, extended his hand and the two grizzled old warriors embraced and banged hands on each other's backs. Soon, all the others had gone to their beds and only Erwin and Owain remained, sitting companionably by the still glowing embers of the great fire.

'Owain my friend', the village chieftain remarked as he took another gulp from his alepot, 'I have not travelled as widely as you, but I have, in my youth seen much of this island, but even in the great houses of kings, I have not seen entertainment such as this evening's. Those young people are not just travelling entertainers, they have to be Mona trained Bards, and you my friend are no simple bodyguard, nor no travelling player neither. In fact I think I know who you are. You are Owain the Gladiator, who until lately trained the warriors of Mona. You could have defeated me easily in that wrestling tonight, and I thank you for enabling me to end this evening on a happy note. But if you and your son are here with a lady who bears all the marks of a high ranking Druid, and young people of rare talents, I am guessing that Lord Myrthin does not expect Mona's defence against the Romans to succeed and wishes to save the talent of these young people to be saved. If you are sent, they must indeed be important.'

Owain took a moment to decide what to do. Either he trusted the cunning old chieftain or he must kill him now and take his charges away, adding to his list of enemies.

'My friend you may only be a local chieftain, but you have the perception and awareness that put to shame many a King or Druid. You are right. Lord Myrthin fears that the many talents of these young people will be lost forever, if they are still on Mona when the Romans arrive there, He asked me to spirit them away in this way, because we know have another enemy, Lord Maelgwyn, who would kill or capture our charges for his own proposes'

At the name of Maelgwyn, Erwin spat copiously into the fire,

'If you are Maelgwyn's enemy, then you are forever my friend. He has enticed too many of my young warriors away, and none have yet returned, but be warned, he is a dangerous and spiteful opponent with powers far beyond those given to most of us. In the morning I will give you fresh provisions and set you on a road that should help you avoid the clutches of Maelgwyn's men. However from what I have seen tonight, those men had best be ready for what they will face.'

Owain gulped down the last of his ale and replied.

'Lord Erwin, you have not seen one quarter of what our enemies will face if they take on this group of travellers!' With this the two old warriors downed the last of their ale and went laughing off to bed.

Chapter 5

The morning brought a veil of fine, soaking rain sweeping in from the west on a chill breeze, as the small group of travellers swiftly ate hot bannocks and downed cups of warmed and honeyed ale. Packing their fresh provisions into their packs and wrapping their cloaks around them, they set off, blessed by by some cheery words from Erwin and his smiling wife. Only a few minutes out from the village, Alwyn spurred his pony forward alongside Owain.

'Owain, you should know that there is one back there at the village who wishes us harm. I felt his hatred early on in our visit, and eventually I was able to identify the one who bore us ill will. He was a tall, thin, ill favoured youth called Tammoch. I could not find out why he hated us, but this morning I know he left the village even earlier than us, and I believe that he is taking what he knows to Maelgwyn!'

Owain swore under his breath.

'Thank you for that information Alwyn, I will not even ask you how you know it. Erwin told me that he regarded Maelgwyn as an enemy, one who sometimes stole away Erwin's young warriors, with promises of wealth and power no doubt. It may be that this Tammoch was Maelgwyn's spy in the village, primed to look out for us. Well, within two days, Maelgwyn will know where we have been, and will make a guess at our journey plans for the next few days. There are few enough passes through these mountains. However, it will take him at least two days more to prepare, provision and send a war band to intercept us. We must push on as fast as we can, avoiding settlements and try to get ahead of him'. Alwyn looked thoughtful.

'I feel sure that somehow I will know when Maelgwyn is told, he will not be able to guard his thoughts then, maybe I can even discover his plans. One thing I now know, no one will be able to take us by surprise, and no one with evil intentions towards us can hide them from me, not even Maelgwyn!'

The old gladiator broke into a rare smile and clapped Alwyn on the back with such a heavy hand that the slightly built youth nearly fell from his pony. Alwyn dropped back to tell the others his news whilst Lorchar spurred forward to hear it from Owain.

Later that day they had stopped to eat in a secluded valley. The rain had mercifully stopped and now the midday sun was warming the valley through the trees, causing a mist to rise up through the leaves. The younger members of the party were sitting around together eating their fill of oat bannocks and cheese. As they discussed the news, the different aspects of their characters would have been evident to any observer. Garth had taken it calmly, confident that it if it did come to a fight, he and his father, with the backing of the others would be more than a match for any war band.

'Let them come, with young Alwyn here to prevent a surprise attack, we can prepare and defeat whatever Maelgwyn throws at us, Maelgwyn only has one warrior worthy of the name and Carreg is a hothead, no match for me or Father'.

Pered, as always was full of cold fury. 'We should have chased that slack jawed idiot, Tammoch. With Branwen here to guide me through the forest, I could have caught up with him easily and stopped his blabbing forever'

Branwen hugged her knees with excitement that the haughty Pered had taken note of her talents and was including her in his schemes, but suddenly a new thought entered her head, and almost beyond her will she spoke words that she had not planned.

'Pered, soon you will realise that you of all people need no one to guide you through the forest, and at a speed that no man can match'

Pered and the others excitedly questioned Branwen on her statement, but indeed she was not able to expand on it, she hardly understood where it had come from herself and resolved to speak to Lorchar about it later. Cerna spoke with that gentle, honeyed voice that always seemed to calm situations.

'Already, it seems to me, that we are daily learning new things about ourselves. Alwyn's news about this boy and Maelgwyn is unwelcome, but the fact is, we know about it, and it is certainly a comfort to me to know that, thanks to Alwyn and his amazing talents, no one can ever surprise us with evil intent. I am not without some powers myself and sometimes I get glimpses in my dreams, aspects of the future that always come to pass, and I see us feasting in a great king's hall many weeks from now, beyond any danger from Maelgwyn. I am not saying that we will not meet danger and hardship, but I am saying that as far ahead as I can see we will come through it intact'

The thoughtful Alwyn who had held his counsel until now, spoke his words of advice. 'Thank you, Cerna for those words, and I pray they may come true, but remember, these glimpses some of us have into the future, are sometimes signs of what can come to pass if we all do the right thing, and for now the right thing is for all of us to stick together and make our decisions according to the Truth. I believe the fates have more in store for us than than Maelgwyn and his pack of ne'er do wells can ever imagine. Cerna is right, each day we learn more and more about our powers, and as yet, we have not even had the training from great old Druids that this journey will bring.'

Garth laughed gently. 'I am a simple warrior like my father. I watch and listen to you, my friends with amazement. I have not developed any new powers on this journey as yet, though I now know that I would use the skills I do have to defend you all to the death. I am sure that you have the powers and the character to help us keep the fire of our culture alive as the Roman wind sweeps through this land, and as long as I am able I will help you do it'

Again something seemed to take over Branwen's mind and make her say something she had never thought before,

'Garth, the journey will be a long one and we have barely started. You will find that you are able to access powers that you never knew you had, powers that, as long as you continue to use them for good, will make you the mightiest warrior in all of Britain!'

All these revelations and bold statements from young people not normally given to speaking to each other as though they were experienced court Druids, seemed to leave them all stunned and silent, and slowly they all drifted off, back to their ponies, ready to ride on, but with much to think on.

A day and a half later and much further north and west, Tammoch reached Maelgwyn's dismal mountain fastness in a high, rocky valley with sentries on all the approaches. He was stopped by heavily armed guards a long way outside the heart of Maelgwyn's well defended estate. Luckily for him, Tammoch had remembered the safe words he was to give if he had news for Maelgwyn. He stammered them out, shaking with fear at the fierce appearance of of the ex-druid's warriors, with their limed hair and facial tattoos. Soon the young man was kneeling before the unblinking gaze of the notorious warlord.

'So, Tammoch of Lord Erwin's clan, you bring me news I think?'

Still shaking with fear, Tammoch replied with a stammer in his voice that brought a guffaw of rough laughter from the senior warriors assembled in Maelgwyn's hall.

'M-my Lord I d-do. I had heard that you were looking for a party of young people accompanied by an old warrior and a young one. Just such a group turned up at our village a few days ago. Some of the young ones were skilled bards despite their youth. Indeed, I have never heard better and the two warriors were exceptional and bested all our strongest warriors in contest. The old one wore his hair like a Roman and I heard him named Owain, his son, a huge, and powerful youth was called Garth. In addition to these, and the three bards there was a young woman who seemed to be their expert on healing and a woman of middle years who carried weapons like she knew how to use them and carried herself as one used to command.'

Maelgwyn, smiled, stroked his beard and replied in a calm voice. 'You have done well young man, in truth, you are not made by nature to be a warrior, but you have a quick mind and a good memory for those essential facts that can mean much to a leader. You will make a good messenger, and perhaps, with training, a scout. These are indeed the ones I seek. Now, can you tell me the direction they were heading?'

'Indeed sir, they were heading south and west. From our village, following the valley, most travellers are heading for the mountain pass that will take them to the West coast.'

Another smile crossed the face of Maelgwyn at this news. 'Excellent! I feared they would head east into areas where I have, as yet, little influence. Now, if we are quick, we can cut them off and capture them. However, it will take at least a day to gather together the men and provisions for such a move, and we must not delay. Tammoch, after you have eaten and rested for a short while, I will give you a fresh horse, and a warrior who knows the way, and you shall go to see some friends of mine in the mountains they must pass through. Indeed, you will need this companion, for without him, these men of the hills would just cut your throat. By profession they are killers and thieves who prey on those who must travel through the pass you speak of. They must be told that if they kill the others and bring me, alive and well, the boy called Alwyn, they will be suitably rewarded.'

At this point, Maelgwyn suddenly grasped at his head with both hands, and stumbled forward from his stool, so that he knelt on the floor, muttering and groaning. In alarm his warriors rushed forward, grasping their sword hilts. Two of them roughly grabbed Tammoch, fearing he had brought poison, or was the instrument of magical intervention. By this point Maelgwyn had recovered and laughed in a rather strained way.

'No, no, it is nothing. I was merely overcome by excitement and gave myself a sudden headache. Let the boy go. He needs to prepare for his journey. Gerlon, you accompany him, you were a member of that band of cut-throats until a year ago. Carreg, you go and put together a troop of, say, twenty five of your best warriors and have them provisioned for a week's journey. If the mountain men fail, it will be down to you to kill what is left of this band of heroes, and bring the boy, alive and unharmed to me. Understood?'

The tall warrior smiled his merciless grin and nodded. Gerlon, a wiry unkempt young man with a scarred face led Tammoch away and the rest of the warriors rushed off, leaving Maelgwyn alone with the saturnine Bran. It was the second in command who spoke first.

'My lord, what happened just then?. Your story may have fooled the others but not me, I have never seen you affected like that before. Was it the boy?'

'Sometimes Bran, you are too quick for your own good. Yes, it was the boy. Somehow, as soon as I was threatening their well being, he was aware of it, and probed my mind in a way that it has never been touched before. I was unprepared for it, and and that was a mistake I will never make again. However, you can be sure that the boy will never be taken by surprise. I now even doubt whether that bunch of undisciplined outlaws in the mountains can win an encounter with a combination of Alwyn's mind and the fighting skills of Owain and Garth. They are bound to do some damage though, and then it will give Carreg and his boys a chance to catch them up. Two warriors, a woman and some half grown children including bards and a healer can be no match for Carreg and twenty five hardened warriors. Anyway, now you see why I am desperate to capture this boy. Without training he can hurt me in a way no other Druid except perhaps Myrthin himself can do. If we are to seize the advantage I want from the Romans taking Mona, I must have the boy under my control.'

Maelgwyn's chief adviser bowed and said he understood perfectly, but his grey, intelligent eyes glittered a little as he saw other possible scenarios emerging from the days and weeks ahead.

Chapter 6

The band of travellers were preparing camp in the wooded hills when Alwyn got his presentiment of danger. He knew where it was coming from and immediately sought out Maelgwyn in his mind. He caught the ex-druid unawares and probed deeply and painfully into Maelgwyn's mind, seeing all his plans in a moment, before Maelgwyn was able to respond and close his mind to the attack. Alwyn calmly called the others around and told them of what had occurred. Owain could scarcely believe it, but by now had learned to trust the slender young man with his pale blue eyes and confident stare. He turned his mind to the practicalities of an impending fight.

'Will you be able to tell where and when we are to be attacked Alwyn?' The young man pursed his lips and thought for a moment.

'You must realise that I do not fully understand my powers as yet. It does seem though, that anything that threatens my wellbeing, or that of those I care about, sets off an alarm within my mind and I seem to see more clearly what the nature of the threat is and where it is coming from. I believe that I will be able to tell when the threat will come, but as to where, this country is new to me and I have no names or words to tell where that threat will be. However I think I will be able to see our would be attackers with enough clarity to describe the countryside they are waiting in with plenty of detail.'

'That will be enough I think. I know this country well and I know where I would mount an attack from. If you can describe it, I know I will recognise it. We will be outnumbered, by dangerous and desperate men, But they will not be warriors, and they will be expecting the attack to be a surprise. If we are ready for them, we can give them a shock they will long remember, those that survive.' That last phrase was added by Owain with such a grunt of determined ferocity that Alwyn looked at him with new eyes. He knew that Owain was an expert in his field, he knew that in his day the man had been one of the greatest of gladiators, only now did he have an insight into what that might mean. Soon he would understand it even more.

Late into the evening Owain led the others in a discussion about how they would deal with this new threat and what the role of each of them would be. When the others had been told to go and get some sleep, the three experienced fighters, Owain, Garth and Lorchar stayed up later, talking quietly amongst themselves. Owain took it upon himself to sum up what had been decided.

'So, we are agreed, Branwen is safe enough, she can, in the end, simply disappear so that not even the most skillful hunter could find her; Pered is inexperienced but with his amazing speed and ferocity he should be more than a match for any wild outlaws; our concern must be Alwyn and Cerna, they have amazing powers but they are no warriors. Skillful with the bow they may be, but they are vulnerable in hand to hand fighting, and they are of course, our most important future Druids. So when battle is joined tomorrow or the next day, Garth and I will do the majority of the fighting, though if you and Branwen could kill or disable a couple of their men each, Lorchar, and then fall back to ensure the safety of Alwyn and Cerna, I believe we will be doing all we can to ensure we move on from this to next challenge'

Lorcha smiled sadly 'For the sake of the future of our culture in Britain, I hope you are right Owain!'

They travelled on all the next day and it was late afternoon when Alwyn quietly called Owain to a stop. They were now in very different country from the wooded hills and well tended fields of the previous day. Now they were in a steep and rocky valley overlooked by towering mountains, thick with gorse, and birch on the lower slopes, bare stones, slick with dew, and twisted, stunted oaks and yew, punctuated the bracken covered higher slopes. It was a forbidding landscape, and Alwyn's quietly spoken words did little to lift the mood.

'They are waiting for us, not too many miles ahead. Twelve to fifteen of them armed with long knives and spears. They do not fear us. Their leader thinks he should be able to deal with an old man and an untried youth, saving your presence gentlemen. Indeed he is a large and ferocious looking gentleman. Oh, and Tammoch is with them though he is terrified. There is one of Maelgwyn's warriors there too, he seems familiar with the outlaws. They are waiting in a narrow wooded valley with cliffs on either side, just round a sharp bend, so that we will come on them suddenly. They have not bothered to hide anyone in the woods, thinking to frighten us with their numbers'

Owain looked grim but determined as he called to the others and laid again out his plan of action, but in more detail. Branwen had travelled ahead to spy out the lie of the land. Soon she came back to the main party to describe what she had seen.

'They are around the next bend, spread across the path. They are expecting us soon and seem confident of success. The leader is called Arcod, and he has his information from Maelgwyn's man, Gerlon. They will rely very much on Arcod's confidence I think'

'Very well. Leave the ponies here, Garth and I will lead, Lorchar, Branwen and Pered behind and Alwyn and Cerna at the rear. Have your weapons ready but use them only when I begin'

Owain slipped off his pony and took his great oak staff in hand, his cloak hiding his Roman sword. Garth shouldered his great axe and felt for the long Gaulish knife at his belt. Lorchar and Branwen ensured their many throwing knives were loose in their sheaths and Pered stroked the boar spear with clear excitement. Nervously, Alwyn and Cerna nocked an arrow each in their bows, and they set off round the bend.

They were greeted with raucous laughter as they came in sight of the brigands. Arcod straightened his knife belt and took a firmer grip of his spear as he stepped out in front of the others. He was tall and strong looking with a cruel smile on his face as he spoke.

'I am afraid we must detain you fine ladies and gentlemen. You are passing through our territory now and you have things we want'

Owain and Garth walked forward within a pace of Arcod and his immediate henchmen. Owain leaned heavily on his staff and replied in a bold voice.

'Indeed, which of the chiefs of the Ordovices do you owe allegiance to? I know them all well, and the King too.'

'Their writ does not run in these mountains, we make our own laws here, and all must pay to use this pass' The words slipped from Arcod's mouth with a slimy layer of contempt on them as he looked the travellers up and down.

'So you are outlaws then, well I am sure we can come to some sort of arrangement to allow us to pass Arcod' Owain threw the outlaw leader's name in and watched with some satisfaction the look of shock on the man's face.

'So you know my name Owain of Mona, I am flattered but I am afraid there is no room for bargaining. We will take all we want and that includes the boy Alwyn. Is that him cowering there at the back?'

'We know much more than you can imagine Arcod. For example, that you are working for Maelgwyn, and that you got your information from Tammoch and Gerlon. Did they tell you that all this party with the exception of my son and I are Druids? Do your men know the penalty for even threatening a Druid? That penalty extends into the next world as well as this one. So have a care!'

There was no laughter now, just anxious looks from amongst the superstitious mountain men, but Arcod was made of sterner stuff.

'Your Druids will soon have no more power to threaten us poor folk. The Romans will destroy them. In the world that comes, powerful men who seize the initiative will be the ones to be associated with. Men such as Lord Maelgwyn. So your threats mean nothing to us old man. We will kill those who fight us and take as slaves those who submit. The two young girls will be particularly welcome in these lonely hills!'

Garth noticed that his father's knuckles tightened with anger at these words, and he tensed for imminent action. Owain shrugged and seemed to slump slightly, causing him to change the grip on his staff. The brigands took it as a sign of an old man's weakness, but Garth knew better. In a moment the outlaws would discover what they had done.

Suddenly, the heavy oak staff, with its metal ends, transformed itself in the hands of the old gladiator into a deadly weapon. In a split second, the bottom end of it had been swung upwards with huge force into the fork of Arcod's straddled legs. Before his grunt of pain was over, the great staff crashed down on his skull, smashing it open. As the man to Arcod's left reached for his knife, the heavy metal tip of the staff smashed into his mouth and nose, but he felt no pain, because in a moment, Garth's huge axe had severed his head from his body. In one movement, Owain threw down the staff, drew his sword and plunged it into the chest of the man that stood on Arcod's right. Simultaneously, Garth swung his axe again, and almost split the next outlaw in two. Lorchar threw two daggers at the same time, lodging in the throats of two of the brigands, who were charging forward. With an excited shout, Branwen disappeared, and a man screamed, as a dagger was plunged into his back. Pered gave a great yell, and moving at a speed that was difficult to follow, charged the outlaws, killing two with the boar spear before they understood he was amongst them. Not to be outdone, Alwyn and Cerna let go a flurry of arrows, incapacitating three of the rear ranks of of mountain men, though not before they had hurled a volley of rocks at the young Druids, one of which struck Alwyn a blow on the temple which knocked him senseless. The two remaining outlaws dropped their weapons and fled into the trees. Tammoch and Gerlon, who had been sitting watching events from horseback, wheeled their mounts around and galloped off. Cerna dropped to her knees to tend to a groaning Alwyn staunching the the blood form the wound on the boy's temple with her fine woollen dress

Unaware of the incident behind them, and in their excitement, Branwen and Pered wanted to pursue the escaping men, but Lorchar restrained them.

'It is no part of the task of a Druid to kill unless absolutely essential to save your own life, or that of others. Certainly, bloodlust is not seemly in those of our calling'

She said this with a meaningful look at the two hotheads. Then Branwen noticed Alwyn lying bleeding on the ground and a distraught Cerna trying to help. With a yell of horror she rushed back to Alwyn's side and took out her belt pack of herbs and dressings. She had cared for people with far worse injuries than this many times before, so she was astonished at the panic she felt that something might have happened to damage Alwyn. Her heart beat faster and her breath was hard to control as she tried to say reassuring things to the young Druid whilst dressing his wounds. It was at this point that she realised that her largely solitary life as a child in the forest with her mother meant that she had developed few friendships. Now this small group of people, many of whom she had not known long, meant a great deal to her, and maybe this quiet, intelligent young man with his intense eyes and willing smile meant more to her than she had been prepared to admit. Tears were flowing down her face at this point and a slight blush at these hitherto unrealised feelings coloured her cheeks.

Soon Branwen was greatly relieved to see Alwyn' eyes flicker and open slightly as a little colour returned to his skin. The boy shook his head as if to clear it, and gave a broad and encouraging smile at the worried face of Branwen. By this time Owain and Garth had finished the unpleasant task of putting out of their misery the wounded brigands. Cleaning his blade carefully Owain spoke seriously to the worried young Druids.

'An important lesson has been learned today I think. Alwyn, whilst you have the valuable skill of being able to predict the intentions of an enemy, it is well for you to learn today, at our first encounter, that in a fight, not all that happens is intended. People are frightened, unskilled, hot blooded. Stones, arrows and spears fly around dangerously, swords and axes are wielded wildly. So, my young friends, despite your special skills, you will still need to keep your wits about you at all times, just like the rest of us!'

'Lorchar gave wise advice to some of you just now. Today we have won a great victory and those that escape will tell the story in such a way that others will begin to fear us. I must caution you all against the danger of taking pleasure in killing. It will eat away at your soul. Also, we will have more dangerous enemies to fight than these cut-throats, so beware of over confidence. Now let us collect our ponies and move quickly away from this god forsaken place'

Several hours later, and many hundreds of feet lower, the party were camping in a secluded forest glade, and preparing to rest up for the night after their meal. Most of the younger members of the party, Pered and Branwen in particular, were still excited about that day's victory over such dangerous seeming foes. However Owain and Lorchar were anxious about the danger of over-confidence, and so spoke about the imminent danger of Carreg and his warriors. Owain began.

'Look, I understand your need to celebrate the victory we enjoyed today. Most of you have not faced mortal danger before, and you all handled it brilliantly well. You must know though, that the danger is not yet over. Maybe as soon as tomorrow, Carreg and his men will be upon us. These are not desperate, untrained criminals, such as we fought today. They are a large party of well trained warriors, led by a skillful and ruthless leader, working to the direct command of a most powerful and merciless lord, who will not forgive failure. Even with my experience I am struggling to work out how we can defeat them when we are so few!'

The younger members of the party looked at each other fearfully. Even Garth was shocked by the bleak outlook his father had shared with them. It was Lorchar who came up with a plan.

'Well we are few indeed, and although brave, most of you are inexperienced in battle. However, we do have one advantage, one element of surprise. Five of us are Druids now, and no ordinary Druids either. We have powers that can be used to shock and terrify the simple warriors that are sent against us. Remember, although they work for Maelgwyn now, all of them were brought up to respect and even fear the power of the Druids, so if we play it right we can reduce their numbers and willingness to fight early in our meeting with our enemies'

Pered, with his usual impetuosity, dared to interrupt, albeit respectfully. 'But Lady Lorchar, we have seen something of the powers of the rest of us, but apart from your amazing fighting skills, what other powers do you possess that will frighten these warriors.'

'Indeed Pered, Only Branwen knows my secret, but it is right that you all find out now, so that it does not shock you as much as it will our enemies. Owain, this will challenge your rather matter of fact view of the world, I am afraid, so prepare to re-evaluate how you see the spirit world and Druids. The rest of you should know that I am in complete control of what will happen next and you should fear nothing.'

With this Lorchar stood up and shook herself, and raised her hands to the sky as her eyes went back in her head and a strange sound come from her lips, between a moan and a growl. Suddenly the air around her seemed to vibrate in a strange way and became like mist over a lake. Then to the utter shock of everyone except Branwen, who hugged her knees with the joy of knowing, when others did not, a large grey wolf sprang from the disturbed air, growling and snarling, ears back and teeth bared. All sprang back in shock, and instinctively Owain and Garth put their hands to their daggers, as Branwen shouted to them to hold their hands, that what they saw was indeed Lorchar, with the spirit of the she wolf called to the fore. In a moment there was another perturbation of the air and before them stood Lorchar, only stark naked and laughing at the reaction of the others to her transformation. She picked up her tunic from the ground and shrugged it on.

'Oh! I am truly sorry my friends, even with my warning, I seem to have shocked you there. Only Branwen has any experience of witnessing the absorption of the spirit of a wild creature into a human, and I am sure that none of the rest of you have ever seen it occur. It is a gift that is given to very few, and needs to be used sparingly or else the spirit of the creature will slowly prevail. I did not mean to shock you so greatly, but imagine what the effect will be on simple men, already in fear of our powers!'

Owain was sitting again and shaking his head. 'I had heard of such things of course, but thought them old wives' tales. I never thought to see such a transformation myself, and from someone I count as a friend. You are right Lorchar, what I have seen makes me re-evaluate all I believed until now. I always knew that Druids stood for what was right in the world, Truth, respect for Nature, talking before fighting and so on, but I confess that I always thought the rest was just smoke and mirrors, to convince the peasants that they had powers to back up what they preached. You people have made me see that I underestimated you!'

Lorchar replied.'Good! Now our plan must be to use the special abilities we have, to unsettle and frighten off the weaker and more susceptible members of Carreg's band before we have to fight the rest. I will rehearse you all in some of the longer and more terrifying curses to be used on those who threaten Druids. I know you all have your own ways of making them even more effective. Alwyn, if you can give Owain plenty of warning of the timing and disposition of any attack, I am confident he can use his experience to come up with a strategy to defeat them. Though be warned, we may not come out of it as relatively unscathed as today'

The young Druid touched his bandaged head and smiled gently as he formulated his response.

'Already I can tell you that they are not many miles behind us, and their plans are to get ahead of us, and ambush us in a place where it would be difficult for us to escape. As soon as Carreg thinks of how he is going to position his men, I will know of it. I expect we will be meeting them by midday tomorrow'

'Excellent!' Owain rubbed his hands in anticipation. 'I wish I had always had such intelligence before a battle. Many lives could have been saved. Well, as soon as Lorchar has taught you these curses we had all better try to get some sleep. Meanwhile Garth and I have some preparation to do. We may not have your powers, but we too can give Carreg and his men some surprises.'

Somehow or other, the party did all eventually get some sleep. Alwyn woke early as his mind picked up Carreg's early start and conversations with his lieutenants. He swiftly dressed, and went to find Owain. He found the old warrior sat by the banks of a stream, stripped to the waist with Branwen standing behind him, scraping off the long white hairs that covered his shoulders and back with a razor sharp knife, while Garth sat nearby grinning and sharpening a long sword. Owain got up and turned round to greet him, and Alwyn was amazed at the transformation. Gone was the grizzled beard, and the balding head was covered with a leather cap. Owain's broad chest had been scraped clean of the grey hair that normally covered it in a thick mat. Instead, the chest, shoulders and arms were coated in oil, that accentuated the powerful muscles, that had been pumped up by early morning exercise. Owain wore only a short, Roman style leather tunic, leather shin guards and great leather wrist bands. On his belt hung a long British sword, and a wicked looking Gaulish hunting knife, more than a foot long. He pulled on a boiled leather breastplate that seemed to accentuate his powerful physique. He grinned at Alwyn's astonished face.

'Well, I hope Carreg reacts like you! This is my own bit of magic you see. Carreg last saw me four years ago, and will have been telling all his men that I am a past it old greybeard. When they see me, they will have moments of doubt about Carreg, and I hope he will have moments of doubt about his view of me. He will certainly have been preparing to fight someone who favours the short Roman sword and a small shield. Instead, I will fight him with the long British sword and the Gaulish knife. Believe me I am equally effective with either, and an element of surprise is always useful. By the time Carreg actually fights me, his confidence will be shaken just enough to give me quick victory. And quick is what I need it to be, my stamina is not what it used to be and a long fight would be risky. Well boy, what have you to tell me?'

Alwyn shook his head briefly took a deep breath and began. 'Carreg and his men have already set off, they should be past us in an hour or so, and the plan is to find a piece of ground with trees on either side of the road, so that two archers can hide on each side to pick us off at a signal from Carreg. He plans to defeat you in single combat, so that the rest of us will be disheartened. His two main lieutenants will take out Garth, and the rest will rush forward to overpower us, without risk to me. They want to take the two girls alive too, for reasons that I do not need to explain. Once they have found the place they are looking for, I will know of it and will be able to tell you more about dispositions'

'Excellent, they are overconfident, as I expected. They will find our planned surprises quite a shock I think' Owain rubbed his hands and flexed his massive shoulders, but then he whipped round as he heard an explosion of pure anger from the normally relaxed Garth.

'Those swine dare to think of treating Druids like that! If one of them even puts one hand on Cerna . . . or Branwen for that matter, they will have me to answer to!'

'So, that is the way things lie is it?' breathed Owain. 'Listen son, I understand how you feel, but later today you must channel that anger into cold focussed rage. Hotheadedness could cost you your life, and without our combat skills, people you care about will have much less chance of survival. So sit for a moment or two, and reflect, decide how you will deal with a two man attack on you by skilled and experienced warriors, and be able to go on and deal swiftly with others. If we do this right, and I can quickly deal with Carreg, I think we could quickly have them in disarray.'

Everyone in the party was now up and about, and they broke their fast, and set about making their preparations for the ordeal ahead. The younger members of the party were divided in their reaction to what faced them that day. Pered and Branwen were excited, though they felt that frisson of fear, knowing, though hardly believing, that death that day was a possibility. Alwyn and Cerna, both less inclined to relish combat, were nervous and found eating difficult, though they knew they needed the energy the food would give them. They had not enjoyed the the feelings that the previous skirmish had left them with, never having believed that they, as Bards and Druids should have to even contemplate taking lives. They quietly discussed their feelings with each other and with an understanding Lorchar, who left them convinced that the fates had left them no choice and that the action they were embarking on was at one with the Truth, and the circle of right actions. Garth kept himself to himself but was clearly maintaining that sense of righteous fury he had felt earlier, along with his realisation of his hitherto unspoken, strength of feeling about Cerna, and was, as his father had advised, channelling it into a a cold rage that augured very poorly for any opponents who might face him later in the day. Owain and Lorchar spent some time in quiet conversation, earnestly planning how things would go later that day.

Eventually, Alwyn went very quiet and his pale face turned whiter, his brows twisted in concentration, and his deep blue eyes seemed focussed elsewhere. The others gathered round, and sat on the ground to await his words. After what seemed an age, he spoke.

'Well, it seems the trap is laid, they are about half an hour ahead on the south west road. They wait at the crown of a small hill, two archers in the woods on either side. They have hidden their horses over the brow of the hill, with Tammoch, who they think useless for fighting, looking after them. They are in good spirits and expect few losses. many of them, though not Carreg, or his lieutenants, Gerlon who we have seen before and another whose name I have not learned, spent many hours drinking last night and I think not all are clear headed today'

'So, the time has come my friends!' Owain spoke with grim determination. 'This will be a difficult and frightening day, but you hear what our young friend says, many of these brave warriors have been taking drink. Not unknown before a battle, but strange when they outnumber us so greatly in numbers, age and experience. Believe me, despite their fear of Maelgwyn and the confidence building boasts of Carreg, many of these men are worried about attacking Druids, and who knows, maybe a few are afraid of the possibility of facing Garth or I in battle. Well, we know what to do to raise their fears higher. From the time we get back to the south west road, we move quietly, Alwyn will warn us when we are near. From that point, we leave the ponies and Lorchar and Branwen will move into the woods to do what they must do. We will advance, and hope to keep Carreg talking for a little while, until Lorchar and Branwen rejoin us and then we will institute the plan laid out by Lorchar last night. The rest is in the hands of fate, and the gods and spirits you are more familiar with than I'

For a little more than half an hour the small group moved quietly down the broad hill path that passed through forest and river, the morning sun gradually warming up. Then Alwyn raised his hand and whispered urgently.

'They await us round the next bend, the two archers on the right are hiding close together in a hazel thicket thirty bow lengths from the road and the two on the left behind adjoining beech trees some twenty five bow lengths in but slightly raised up.'

At this, all of them slipped silently from their ponies, tied them up and arranged their weapons. Branwen and Lorchar slipped silently into the forest, the older Druid with a look of grim determination on her face, Branwen with her usual impudent grin. The rest marched on up the road together, Owain and Garth a few paces in front of the others. Around the bend, on a rise in the road stood a large band of men, some with iron helmets some with shields, all with spears, or swords drawn. There was an outburst of mutters and whispers from the warriors when the small band of travellers appeared, but it was silenced by a fierce look from the young man at the front with limed up hair and colourful cloak and trousers. Owain and Garth walked up and stopped about twenty paces from Carreg, the others remained five paces behind. Owain placed his arms akimbo and looked up and down the assembled warriors with an expression of immense contempt.

'Well Carreg my boy, do you think you have brought enough soldiers to tackle an old man, an inexperienced warrior, a woman and some children? I thought you had a reputation for courage?'

Carreg looked annoyed at Owain's words and more than a little perplexed at the change in Owain's appearance and the obvious preparedness of his opponents, but he tried to hide these emotions in bluster and threat.

'It seems that the Lord Owain has benefited from travelling with a Druid, she has obviously used her witchcraft to make you appear younger than the last time I saw you four years ago. Where is the witch and her familiar, the girl Branwen?

'Yes, I remember you well from four years ago lad. I remember every fault in your fighting technique, brave, but stupid I recall. As for the Lady Lorchar and Branwen, well they are otherwise engaged just now.'

Too late, Carreg saw how he been outflanked, and turned to shout a warning to his archers. Two screams came from the woods on the right, followed by the chilling sound of a lone wolf howling. From the left a shout and a stifled yell followed by the weird banshee wail of the wildcat. The warriors behind Carreg looked at each and some muttered words to ward off evil. Carreg swore at them and glared a threat. Owain shrugged sympathetically. 'The forest can be such a dangerous place in these hills I find.'

As he spoke, Lorchar appeared from the undergrowth adjusting her knife belt and there appeared to be fresh blood on her face. Branwen just appeared out of nowhere on the path beside Lorchar and grinned as she wiped blood from a long and wicked looking dagger.

It was Lorchar who spoke first, with a voice that the others had not heard before, harsh and powerful, it seemed to find its way into every crevice of the brains of the warriors at whom she aimed her words.

'Yes, you are now dealing with Druids, not just me, but everyone of us, except for the Lord Owain and his son, who are under the express protection of the Head Druid and the Council. You will know that Druids, and those they place under their protection, are sacred, and their persons sacrosanct. The penalty for harming them or even threatening to do so is a curse so all encompassing and so dreadful that you will wish you had never heard it.'

Her voice raised itself even louder and higher, and began to describe in the most graphic terms, the death enemies of Druids could expect, the torments their souls would suffer in the afterlife, the curse that would follow their families and descendants for generations. Branwen joined in with a high pitched version that seemed to cut through their very skins. Then they were joined by the powerful tones of Pered, whose great voice vibrated through their chests and made several of them vomit. Cerna began to sing a dreadful dirge that seemed to dig into their very souls, dragging up every sad event in their lives and causing hardened warriors to fall on the floor sobbing. Alwyn remained silent but scanned the ranks of warriors, looking for weakness, and exploiting it ruthlessly. One by one, he entered their minds, and conjured up images of these terrible events and torments, actually happening to the warriors and their families. Several ran away screaming.

Before it was too late, Carreg shook his head violently, as if ridding himself of the awful effect of the curses. He raised his huge sword above his head, and without even bothering to check if anyone was following, charged direct at Owain, screaming at the top of his voice. The screams seemed to snap Carreg's two lieutenants, and several other warriors out of their terrorised trances, and they too charged forward.

Carreg swung a mighty blow at Owain who skilfully parried it with his own sword, but was knocked back a pace by the sheer power of the attack. Perhaps Carreg's fighting brain was affected by the oral assault he and his men were subjected to, but always inclined to hotheadedness in battle, he saw Owain's backward step as his opportunity, and launched a second blow from way above his head. It was a blow that would have cleaved any man in two had it connected, such was its power. However Owain, knowing Carreg, was ready for it. He stepped slightly to the left and knocked the blow aside with the sword in his right hand, then he quickly stepped back in and drove the long Gaulish knife in his left hand into Carreg's unprotected right side. He drove it so hard that it penetrated Carreg's heart and the tall warrior fell to the ground with a scream.

At the same time, Gorlan and Carreg's other lieutenant, made a concerted attack on Garth. The young warrior, still channelling that cold rage from earlier, was in no mood to waste time, stepping to one side at the last moment, he turned and decapitated Gorlan with one fierce blow, almost instantaneously driving his long dagger into the throat of the other warrior. The deaths of their three leaders in a matter of moments, brought the rest of Carreg's men to a sudden, uncertain halt. Then they were assaulted by a human whirlwind called Pered, who, with speed that seemed almost supernatural, was suddenly amongst them stabbing wildly with his great boar spear. At the same time they were terrified by the rapid appearance and disappearance of a screaming Branwen, who who would pop up in front of a warrior from nowhere, stab at his face or chest with a long, wicked looking dagger and then, just as suddenly dematerialise with a wild laugh.

A small group were heading towards Alwyn and Cerna at the rear when Lorchar raced between them, turned and to their utter horror, transformed into a huge slavering she wolf before their eyes. This was too much. It was bad enough to endure terrible curses and fight huge warriors who killed their champion with ease, but these manifestations of Druidic magic were too much for the few remaining members of Carreg's warband. They fled screaming into the forest with terrible curses still ringing in their ears.

Owain, Lorchar and their band of young Druids leaned on their weapons and looked around at the devastation they had wrought. Thirteen bodies lay on the ground and they knew there were four archers lying dead in the forest. Owain was used to such sights of carnage, to some extent, so was Lorchar. Despite his relative inexperience, Garth was raised to be a warrior, so was not disturbed by the terrible sights around him, though the adrenalin of battle was coursing through him, causing his hand to shake. The other youngsters were not faring so well. Pered and Branwen were dancing around together in a kind of giddy over excitement that, Owain knew, would soon have its reaction. Cerna was sobbing and Alwyn was was trying to comfort her, but his eyes were staring at the carnage in a way that suggested it would stay in his mind for a long time. Owain looked across at Lorchar who, having swiftly dressed again, looked back and silently nodded. She knew what needed to be done in circumstances like this, and motioned to Owain to get the young people out of the area fast.

Chapter 7

They had picked up the ponies, and moved three or four miles down the steep track, until they reached a flat track that ran alongside the estuary of a great river. The young Druids were still exhibiting a mixture of talkative over excitement and silent introspection, and Lorchar was scanning the estuary shore for a suitable spot. In due course, she saw an area where the oak forest ended in a shallow beach, and she indicated to the party that they should all follow her. They tied the ponies up to the stunted oaks, and made their way down to the beach, with puzzled expressions and whispered comments.

Lorchar gathered them all around her, while Owain stood slightly to one side as puzzled as the others as to what was in the mind of the powerful Druid. Lorchar spoke in a gentle but determined voice.

'Listen, my friends, you have all done exceedingly well today, I am sure that Lord Owain would say that he could not have won such a rapid victory against such enemies with ten experienced warriors' Owain nodded an enthusiastic agreement but did not speak. Lorchar went on.

'However, Owain and Garth excepted, we are Druids, and that means a great many things must follow from the events of the last few days, and today in particular. As you know, Druids rarely kill, and when we do, we must make recompense to the Gods and spirits that grant us our role and powers. Furthermore, when we use, as we had to today, our special powers to hurt and kill, we must seek forgiveness from the Gods and spirits. We must perform a cleansing ceremony for ourselves, and those in our party who are not Druids, and we must ensure that the Gods and spirits understand that we will not, in our excitement at the power we wield, forget that those powers should only be used in such a way, in rare circumstances.'

By now the young Druids were looking at the ground, and those that had been over excited looked a little shamefaced. Owain and Garth looked at each other and shrugged and shook their heads imperceptibly. Lorchar had not yet finished her speech.

'This place we stand in is excellent for our purpose as it is thrice blessed, with oak forest, and a place where river meets the sea. This is what we must do. We will remove our clothes and enter the water. You will all stand in silence, and try to find those spirits that are closest to you. I know the words that will propitiate the Gods and spirits for our actions today, and if we do this well, and in the correct frame of mind, we will be cleansed in our souls, and no one will suffer thoughts and feelings that can damage the soul as a result of what you have seen and done. When that is complete, we will take the opportunity to also cleanse our bodies of the blood and dirt of today's battle. Is all that clear?'

She looked round at the others, nodded and swiftly removed her clothes and walked into the water to face the shore. Branwen swiftly followed suit, though she could not resist a giggle at the thought of being naked in front of the others. She walked swiftly into the water and stood next to Lorchar, looking at the shore, she was looking forward to seeing the boys take their clothes off. Alwyn had been a Druid the longest, and was familiar with rituals that required the absence of clothing. Besides he was anxious for the cleansing to take away some of the images before his eyes, so he shrugged off his tunic and boots without a second thought, and was glad of the cold awakening given by the waters of the estuary. Cerna and Pered had not taken part in a ritual like this before, but Lorchar's words had the desired effect, so they looked at each other, shrugged and the twins took off their clothes and entered the water. Owain and Garth had not moved, believing that the ritual was only for Druids, but Garth found, to his shame that he could not take his eyes off the beautiful, pale, naked body of Cerna. He was shaken from his reverie by a harsh word from Lorchar, who was bidding the two warriors to hurry up and join them. Owain was about to protest, but realising that it was futile and also that Lorchar was doing the best for the young Druids, he shrugged and began to undress, signalling Garth to to do likewise. Branwen giggled again at the thought of the dignified Owain stripping off in front of them, and she shouted out an encouragement, reminding Owain that it was not the first time she had seen him naked, which made Owain blush, but earned Branwen a sharp elbow in the ribs from Lorchar. The two warriors entered the water together, and Branwen could not decide whether she liked Garth's golden muscular physique better than Pered's lean hard body. Cerna however was blushing furiously, as she had been seen by her brother staring far too intently at Garth.

The initial awkwardness over, Lorchar raised her arms to the heavens and chanted in her rich voice.

'Gods of earth, sun and sky, of moon, sea and river, spirits of the forest and mountain, look upon us, your servants and friends. You know what has passed today and two days ago. You know that those of us granted powers by you to protect the Truth, have used them today to harm and kill those who wished us harm, and those who use your power for ill. Therefore, gods and spirits cleanse us! Let us leave this place today, knowing that you forgive us for our actions and that we will not be punished with evil thoughts and dreams. Let us know that you know, that we did what we did only to protect the Truth. Each of us asks those spirits closest to us to intercede and cleanse us!'

There was silence for a moment, then, in a day of amazing events, the most amazing occurred. First, the clouds broke, and a bright ray of sunlight, the only one in the sky, seemed to fall on the circle of people in the estuary, almost blinding them in its intensity. Then a gentle rumble was heard further down the estuary, and a tidal bore a foot high appeared down stream and made its way at an amazing rate towards them. It hit them and covered them in a wave that smelled of the sea, and was past in a moment. All of the party broke out in an excited chatter as they seemed to feel instantly better, and their nakedness forgotten, they all washed themselves clean of the day's dirt and blood.

The following day brought a cold North West wind, and with little shelter down on the coast, all of the group were up early. After a hurried breakfast they set off south down the coast. The previous night's ritual had cleansed their spirits, but now, tired as they were, they travelled mainly in silence. After a while, the irrepressible Branwen, clearly finding the silence oppressive, urged her pony forward and rode alongside Lorchar, glancing up at her with a quizzical expression on her face. After a few minutes Lorchar sighed, turned to her young companion and spoke.

'Well Branwen, what is it you wish to ask me? It is clear that you almost bursting in your need to find something out from me, and yet, unusually for you, you are holding back from getting the words out. Say what you want to say'.

The damn burst immediately. 'Lorchar, I knew about the . . . the wolf thing longer than anyone else but when I saw you transform, well . . . . Then there was the way you were yesterday when you transformed. You actually were a wolf, the way you killed . . . . I have to say it actually scared me, I was afraid you would not be able to come back, to be the Lorchar we all know and . . . and, well you know what I mean. You know I have never transformed, but I know somehow, that I have that power, but Lorchar, it frightens me. It is clear that as Branwen I could control that change to a creature, but if I then become that creature, how do I come back? What if I like that life better?'

Lorchar pulled her pony closer to the girl's and touched her arm tenderly with a smile on her face.

'I felt sure that you would have that power, and it is right that it should scare you. The gods and spirits grant it to few. The thing is this, whatever others may see, you do not actually become a wolf, or whatever, you merely appear to do so. In fact what has happened is that you are allowing the essential spirit of that creature to inhabit your body. Your mind and spirit remains your own, and your body becomes one with the creature. You have its strength, speed, senses, but your own mind remains in control, you can return to yourself when you please. This happens because the spirit of the creature, I mean in my case the spirit of all wolves, recognised in me something special that links me to the wolf, I do not know what. I first transformed when I was your age, and yes, I was frightened, but exhilarated too. I never felt such power before, and the joy of running with other wolves was very special. However it cost me a great deal, when my secret came out, others in my tribe could not accept me, and nothing the Druids said could change their minds. For all I was a royal princess, I had to leave my people at just seventeen and travel down to Mona with only an old Druid for company. My gift brought me much sadness, but it was a gift from the spirits of the forest, and I would not change it. Which creature do you feel an affinity with Branwen?'

Branwen hesitated a moment before replying. 'The thing is Lorchar, it is all of them. There are days when I feel I could become any creature in the forest. But how if I choose wrong, and then I cannot become the one I am destined to be?

'I do not think that is possible Branwen' Lorchar's voice was low and gentle now. 'Remember that day in the forest, the deer, I thought then that it was Cerrunnos the spirit of all the forest, blessing you. You may well have a power that as far as I know is unique. But to make you feel secure about it, think if there is one creature that above all others you feel an affinity with.

Branwen smiled back 'Well I have always liked the wild cat of the forest. It seems, like me to have a fierce and independent spirit, and like me, it seems to be able to disappear at will'

Lorchar laughed. 'I think the choice is a good one, there were many times in the last few years when I saw more than a passing resemblance to a wildcat in you! Certainly yesterday you fought like one. Tonight, when the others are asleep we will try a transformation. You have nothing to fear, in fact I know you will enjoy the experience. However, I will give you this one word of warning, do not let the spirit of the creature inhabit you for too long, else it would slowly draw you away from your human form. Used for the Truth and used sparingly, the power can do you no harm'

Later that night, when all the others were asleep, Lorchar and Branwen crept away from the campsite and up into the forest, until they came upon a fairly open oak grove. Lorchar quickly taught Branwen the transformation ritual, explaining that the most important thing was for her keep in focus the spirit of the wildcat. They began the ritual and soon Branwen began to feel strange, different somehow. Her vision improved dramatically and she began to be aware of scents and smells in an entirely new way. Suddenly she gave a great shiver, and felt an entirely new awareness of her surroundings. She looked down and saw the splayed paws of the cat on her tunic which lay empty on the ground, and she realised that the transformation had happened, she had become in some sense, the embodiment of the wildcat, whilst retaining completely her awareness of herself as Branwen. She had never experienced such an exciting feeling in her life. She looked across at Lorchar and saw that she was transforming herself into the wolf spirit. Somehow, through their still human souls, they were able to communicate with each other and Lorchar 'told' Branwen that she had said she would enjoy the experience and invited the girl/cat to run with her through the forest in a way that they could never do as pure humans. They ran through the forest and up the hills together for about an hour, with no sensation of tiredness at all. Eventually they reached an open place at the top of the hill a couple of miles from the campsite and sat, enjoying the night as part wolf and part cat respectively. Lorchar sat back on her haunches and gave a great, long howl. Soon she was joined by Branwen who gave the unearthly yowl of the wildcat.

Down by the coast, in the campsite, Alwyn was awakened by the noise and by a strange feeling in his mind. He looked around the sleeping bodies of his companions and saw that Branwen and Lorchar were missing. At first he was alarmed, then he heard that strange, exultant double call again, for a split second he was confused, but then he put all the facts together, and he realised what had happened. In his powerful mind's eye he could actually see the two creatures, wolf and cat sitting together at the top of the hill, exulting in the wildness, and he knew they were happy. He became aware that someone was watching him, and turned to see Cerna sitting up. The girl smiled at him and mouthed the words 'I know too!' at him and they both grinned and went back to sleep.

Eventually Lorchar and Branwen returned to the oak grove, they transformed back again and got dressed, returning to the camp happy but tired. Both were hard to wake for breakfast the following morning. Alwyn took the opportunity to whisper to Branwen 'Cerna and I know what happened last night, and we are happy that you have achieved something so rare and special. It will be our secret until you wish to reveal it to the others' Branwen merely smiled. Alwyn could not help but think there was something cat-like about that smile!

Chapter 8

The next few days of their travels were mercifully uneventful. The trip down the west coast was easy and peaceful and on one evening they spent the night in a small fishing village. In return for music, singing and storytelling they slept in warm rooms after a filling fish stew and good ale.

The next day, as they walked down the well marked path, they emerged from some thick woodland, at the edge of the sea in a pleasant land of rolling pasture filled with sheep and small black cattle. In the distance they saw a large and rugged hill a few miles south of them that stood out from the others by its size and vaguely conical shape. Cerna gave an audible gasp as she saw the hill.

'I am sure that hill is the Carn of Spirits. Our mother came from this area and described it in detail. She was afraid of it and told us never to go there, as it was a place of magic. But that is not the feeling that I am getting as I look at it. I see it as a holy place and it seems somehow welcoming. What do you think Alwyn?'

Alwyn felt a strange, though exhilarating sensation as he looked at the hill. He realised at that moment that it was going to mean something in his life, and soon. Strangely, he felt that at that same moment, someone was looking back at him from that very hill and smiling in anticipation of meeting him. Alwyn was about to tell the others of his feelings when a more unwelcome thought entered his head. He became aware that along the road, waiting for him and his comrades, was a band of armed men. He could specifically see, in his mind's eye, an enormously tall man with long red hair and a gigantic moustache, standing by the roadside, leaning on a large and heavy spear. His companions were less clear, but there were enough to cause them severe problems if they wished. However, despite his fears, he could detect no ill will coming from these warriors, only a sense of a duty being done patiently. Alwyn rode forward to Owain, and told him what he had seen. The old warrior now had great faith in Alwyn's powers, but he told the others, that despite Alwyn's failure to detect any hostility, they should nevertheless be ready for action. He and Garth went to the front of the little column and they both drew their long British swords and hauled their shields from their packs. The others took out their weapons of choice and all felt a slight frisson of fear as they progressed along the narrow roadway, now surrounded by forest once again. Rounding a bend they came in sight of the band of warriors who, spotting them, picked up their spears and swords and blocked the path. Owain rode forward with his right hand raised in the universal gesture of peace, though his sword lay across his knees, ready for action. Owain spoke first.

'Good morning my friends! I assure you we do come in peace, though we are armed for our own protection. Whom do I have the honour of addressing?'

The red haired giant spoke in a deep rumble of a voice. 'I am Lydd, Champion of the Dematae and captain of King Maelor's personal guard. You are now in my King's territory. Who are you?'

Owain decided that in these circumstances the truth might be the best approach. All he had heard of King Maelor suggested that he was a good friend to the Druids and no ally of the Romans.

'I am Owain Ap Emyr, known as Owain the Gladiator, sometime commander of the warriors of Mona. Commanded to visit your King by Lord Myrthin himself. My companions are my son Garth, warrior of Mona, The Lady Lorchar, Pictish Princess and a senior Druid, Alwyn, a Druid of great power, despite his lack of years, Cerna and Pered, bards of great skill and Druids appointed by Myrthin himself and Branwen, Druid and healer of knowledge and skill beyond her tender years. Perhaps you have been expecting us?'

Lydd stared for a moment or two then allowed a great grin to appear beneath the giant red moustache.

'Indeed, Lord Owain, it is an honour to have a warrior of such reknown amongst us. I hope you will share some of your experiences and knowledge with us. Lady Lorchar, your fame as a Druid goes before you. Young Druids, I am sure you will bring much to brighten and enlighten our our simple gathering. Young Garth, you look a fine, well set up young warrior, I am sure that our young bucks will look forward to trying their skills against yours in training combat! Now, if you will accompany us, the hill fort where my lord the King is residing is only a few miles from here and there is an old gentleman waiting there who is most anxious to meet with you all.'

With this he leapt on one of the small, swift ponies the people of this part of Britain used and rode off, his feet almost touching the ground. His band of warriors followed him and the weary travellers rode behind. Soon they came to a great round hill with defensive walls and ditches guarded by more warriors. Eventually, they came through the defensive features and emerged in a wide open field with numerous small huts and one gigantic round house whose doorway was flanked by fifty or more warriors. Emerging from the royal roundhouse was a small rotund man of middle years with a scrawny beard and thinning hair. However, this unprepossessing man wore round his neck a great golden torc and had a sword at his belt, whose hilt was exquisitely worked. His blue woollen cloak of perfect quality was held at the shoulder by a great brooch of wonderfully worked reddish gold and bright silver. This could be none other than King Maelor himself.

He stood before them with his hands on his hips and a broad smile on his face whilst Lydd bellowed out his titles and antecedents in a voice that seemed to shake the hills. Then he spoke in a gentle, intelligent voice.

'Welcome travellers, to this humble hill fort of ours. I wish I could have greeted you at my chief house, but when Huw told me of your your coming, I had had to be here to greet such distinguished guests to my country. Lady Lorchar, it is an honour to receive you. Many years ago I had the honour of meeting your Royal uncle, he was a great man. I have heard much from Huw about how highly Lord Myrthin regards you, and that is enough for me. Lord Owain, your reknown as a warrior and leader of warriors is known throughout this island, we are glad to to receive you here, and perhaps whilst our spiritual friends are engaged in their mysterious business, you and your son would share some military ideas with my warriors and I, since it seems certain that sometime soon we must face the might of the Romans. Young Druids, welcome! My Head Druid, Old Huw is filled with excitement at your coming. We have many Druids here, but none, I am told, with powers such as yours. It seems that three of you are blessed with the talent to entertain, we hope you will find the time to show us those skills. You must all be tired and hungry. You will be shown to where you can wash and rest, and a meal is being prepared for you. If you would join us in my house at noon, we will eat and talk and you can meet Old Huw.'

With this the travellers were whisked off by servants to small houses adjoining the king's house. The men to one house and the women to another. At noon, warriors came to bring them to the royal house. They were seated on benches before great tables facing the door. A large fire was burning in the centre of the house but such was the height of the pointed roof, that the house was neither too hot or at all smoky. A few moments later King Maelor entered with a beautiful fair haired woman on his right arm. She was exquisitely dressed and wore a torc almost as large as the King's, so they guessed that this must be the Queen. On his left side, and a pace or two behind, shuffled a an extraordinary figure, a man almost impossibly old with only a few wisps of long white hair on his head and a long white beard. He was dressed from head to foot in white linen, and his bent body was supported by a thick but twisted black staff with owl skulls hanging from it. His brown face was lined more than any of them had ever seen before, and he clearly had no longer any teeth in his head. However, from this ancient face shone out two incredibly bright blue eyes, sparkling with intelligence and excitement.

The King spoke in his pleasant sing song voice. 'May I present my wife, Queen Delyn.' the queen smiled warmly at each of them and Owain realised, that she was not, as he had first thought a young woman but of a similar age to the King, her beauty was quite exceptional. At this stage the Queen said nothing as the King turned to the ancient man on his left 'And this is my Head Druid, Huw, who was my tutor when I was a child and is now my oldest friend'

It was the old Druid who spoke next. 'At last I meet the young man who I have heard so much about from Myrthin and who has been trying to make contact with me through his mind for the last week. Young man you have an exceptional ability, so far untrained. I am so delighted that I have the opportunity to pass what I know to a worthy student before I leave this world.'

All this was said directly to Alwyn, though he had not been specifically introduced and the young Druid was as keen as the old one to see what could be learned, but Queen Delyn was not about to forget the the niceties of hospitality or pass up the opportunity to to enjoy the other talents of her guests. She spoke in a voice as musical and gentle as the strumming of a harp.

'Come now Huw, tomorrow will do for work, our guests have yet to eat and we have prepared for them, a banquet worthy of such illustrious visitors, and I hope that later we can prevail on some of them to entertain us with the talents we have heard so much about. In these difficult times we have so few opportunities for new amusements in this western outpost and we long to hear of Mona and the adventures they have encountered on their journey'

With this she clapped and the travellers were led to their seats near the King and Queen and the servants began carrying in the feast. It was one of the grandest meals most of them had ever enjoyed, with game, beef and mutton and an endless supply of the delicious mead the Demetae were famous for. Owain leant across to Lorchar as he drank his mead from a fine cup made from Roman Samian ware.'It seems this little kingdom on the edge of Britain is a lot richer than one might expect' he muttered.

Lorchar replied just as softly. 'For all the king's words about fighting the Romans, he does well out of his relations with them. There are gold mines not far from here, run by Roman businessmen and they have much trade that comes and goes from the king's chief village in the east of his lands. A port is growing on the banks of the Towy river, and the Romans protect it from the attacks of the Silures to the east who used to be a major threat to these soft lands of the Demetae.'

Owain grunted 'Aye, the Romans work that way, they make it profitable to be part of their world, then they move in and take over, imposing their laws and taxes. In the lifetime of our young friends here, that little port will become a Roman Fort, and this comfortable kingdom, a client of Rome with no army of its own, and probably no Druids either. I have seen it in Gaul'

Soon the eating was over and Cerna was prevailed upon to sing, with accompaniment from Pered and Alwyn. Within moments, the raucous assembly of rather drunken warriors and farmers and their wives were silenced by the power of Cerna's singing. She held them in the palm of her hand as she had them in tears, and then laughing at a jolly song, then enraptured in some old song of romance. She finished with a rousing song of ancient battles that had the warriors shouting and banging their cups on the tables. This was the perfect time for Pered to step forward to tell some of the old tales. Again his voice held them all enthralled and Old Huw looked at him with new interest and stroked his beard.

After the tales, the entertainment got more raucous and the Queen and her ladies retired. Branwen caused great amusement by treating them to a display of her prowess with throwing daggers around the terrified head of a grizzled warrior, against an upturned table. Garth took on all comers in feats of strength, and the evening was brought to an end by Owain telling tales of his days as a gladiator in Rome.

Many by now had left or fallen into a drunken sleep under the tables. Owain and Lorchar were talking companionably with the King and Lydd whilst Old Huw was drawing the young visitors around him and talking of the next day. The peace was suddenly broken by the door being flung open, and five young warriors in full fighting regalia entering and marching to the king's table. In an instant Lydd and several of his men were over the table, daggers in hand. Owain and Garth were on their feet reaching for their daggers, but the king seemed unperturbed.

'Lord Owain, meet my son Daelor and some of his friends, I apologise for his lack of manners but we do not see eye to eye on a number of matters' he remarked languidly.

The young man at the head of the intruders, who did indeed resemble a younger version of the king though he had his mother's hair colouring, laughed mirthlessly. 'You may lower your daggers Lydd, I mean my father and his guests no harm. I heard that the great warrior Lord Owain was here, and thought I would take the chance to meet him, and let him know that if he was hoping that my father would provide some help to the Druids in Mona, against the Romans, he was likely to be disappointed. You see Lord Owain, my father finds the finer things that the Romans can provide a consolation for losing our freedom and our culture to them, as we will surely do as soon as they have finished subduing the Silures, and destroying the centre of the Druids' learning. Instead, you would do better to give some of your knowledge of fighting the Romans to me, and the band of warriors who have sworn allegiance to me.'

The king had stood up by this point, and although clearly angry with his son, maintained a show of dignified restraint. 'I am afraid my son does not quite grasp the concept of strategic diplomacy. He sees me as a coward for not fighting the Romans now, when they are no threat to me. Indeed they are keeping my ancient enemies the Silures and Ordovices more than busy, so that we are able to concentrate on keeping the pirates from Erin at bay and building up our our wealth, so that when the time comes, as I know it will, when we have to fight the Romans, we can do it from a position of strength.'

The hotheaded young prince was about to speak again when he noticed the slender young Druid with the intense blue eyes staring at him with a strangely powerful gaze. He felt suddenly tired and drained and sat down waving his hand in a vaguely dismissive gesture. Owain looked sharply across at Alwyn who responded with a smile and an almost imperceptible nod. Huw watched this whole unspoken interchange with sparkling eyes and slight smile playing across his lips. Owain cleared his throat and spoke.

'Everyone here knows that I have no love for the Romans, maybe because I know them better than most. However, I also know this, there is no simple way to defeat them, so each of us must deal with them as they see fit. I can show you how they fight, and a few ways to fight them, but remember this, they are rarely defeated for good reason, so deal with them with caution, or you may lose all you care about. Tomorrow, Garth and I will lead a session which will show Lydd and his men a few key tactics. With the King's permission I will extend that invitation to you and your men Prince Daelor, provided I have your oath that you and your warriors will cause no trouble. With respect, Lord Prince, you have enough on your hands if you wish to fight the Romans, you really do not want to upset me as well.'

The King wearily nodded his assent, and the prince, suddenly recovered, rose from his seat. 'You have my word. In the morning then' With that he and his men left as peremptorily as they had arrived.

These events brought the evening to an end and as they walked back to the guest huts Owain laid his arm on Alwyn's shoulder and turned the young man to face him.

'I understand that you looked into Daelor's mind to see his intentions, but there are two things I do not understand. Was it you that made the prince sit down so suddenly and how did you know what I was thinking when I turned to you? I don't want you probing my mind young man'

The young Druid smiled apologetically. 'I am afraid that I am still learning how to control my powers. I entered Daelor's mind with too much force, he is no Lord Maelgwyn. I fear that I may have given him a headache and a strange unsettled feeling. However, although he is a hothead with no love for his father, he genuinely wants to fight the Romans, so will do nothing to disrupt tomorrow's training. As to you, I hope you know that I have too much care and respect for you to ever try to enter your mind without your permission, but the question you asked of me in your head was so powerful, that it came across to me as clearly as if you had spoken it. Our minds must already have the affinity of close friends'

Owain gripped the boy's shoulder and smiled 'I should hope so my boy, I should hope so'

Chapter 9

All too soon the morning light found its way into the guest huts and servants brought hot porridge and ale. Owain and Garth donned their fighting gear and gathered together a stock of training weapons. Lorchar apologised for not accompanying them to the training ground, but stated that her place was with the young Druids to help Old Huw work with them. With this, Huw and some servants, almost as old as he, appeared at the hut, and ushered off the Druids, whilst Owain and Garth went to the flat area outside the enclosed part of the hill fort where the warriors were waiting for them.

For such a very old man, Old Huw set a smart pace as the small party set off through the woods and fields. Soon they came to the rising ground at the foot of a great hill. The hill was purple with heather and green and gold with gorse. A million multi coloured jewels of wild flowers of every hue and shape festooned the hillside. Great, grey rock outcrops dotted the landscape and towards the summit of the hill rocks and scree covered more and more of the ground. Huw pointed upwards.

'This is the Carn of Spirits where the spirits of rock, hill, moor, river and forest meet the spirits of the sea. It is a sacred and holy place for our people, and there, at the top, we will be able, in due course, to speak with those spirits, and find out what they want of us. There too, I will pass on what I know, and friends will pass on what they know, to each of you. I already know that you all have considerable potential, more than you can possibly know, so you will excuse my excitement and a certain amount of impatience!'

The party climbed the increasingly steep hill for the best part of an hour and even these fit young people were breathing hard. They were amazed at the energy of the ancient Druid. In due course they came to a rocky summit and were led to a sheltered area laid out with canopies, furs and cushions, with a great fire blazing and, keeping warm a huge cauldron, from which emanated the tempting smell of a mutton stew. Waiting for them were three others, almost as old as Huw in the ceremonial robes of Druids.

Huw greeted the three Druids with warm embraces and introduced them to his guests. 'This lady is Cerridwen, the greatest healer in the west of this island and perhaps the most treewise Druid of her generation. Today, Branwen, she will work with you and Lady Lorchar. This is Cilmor, Bard and Druid, there is no one, outside of Lord Myrthin himself who knows more about the ancient lore of our people and absolutely nobody who knows more about how to use the words and voices of power, so, Pered and Cerna, he will work with you. Finally, this is my oldest friend Machan from over the sea in Erin. He will help me work with you Alwyn, as he is an expert in the use of some potions that will help us to communicate with the spirits and with each other, young man, in a way that will require the help of another to ensure we return to the right bodies'

With these rather terrifying words he introduced the young Druids to some of the most ancient in all of Britain. Cerridwen spoke first in a voice whose power belied her great age.

'Huw, Huw, you are allowing your enthusiasm to overcome your manners again. You may not require much in the way of sustenance these days but I am sure that these young people do, after the long climb up here.'

She showed the young people to seats beneath the canopy and servants brought them bowls of stew and cups of weak ale. The young Druids and Lorchar talked freely of their recent adventures under the friendly encouragement of the four older Druids, though soon, all were aware just how intently the their new mentors were watching them and listening to their words. In due course, this made them a little self conscious and the tales dried up rather. Cerridwen, who possessed the best social skills of the group, was the first to pick up on this and she rose, rather stiffly, asking Branwen and Lorchar to follow her. They left the summit of the hill and walked for a mile down a steepening valley that led at last to a small oak woodland, and to a fairly open area in its centre. There was a fire lit there and Cerridwen indicated that the others should sit down. She joined them and they sat, silent for a few moments. Branwen looked carefully at the older woman. She would be in her early sixties Branwen guessed, with long, steel grey, curly hair and large dark eyes that always seemed to twinkle with good humour. Her face and arms were very brown from the sun and her face wrinkled, but she seemed remarkably fit, and she exuded a vitality that made her seem much younger than the wrinkles suggested. Cerridwen laughed at the serious study that Branwen seemed to be making of her.

'I suppose that it is only fair that you should stare at me so intently, after the close study of you and your friends we were making at the top of the hill. So, young lady, stare a little longer, and tell me what you see. But this time, look beyond the hair and wrinkles.'

Branwen was rather rocked by these words, which seemed to suggest that Cerridwen had seen what she was thinking. Determined to impress, Branwen emptied her mind of the obvious, and used all her senses to find out more about the friendly Druid. After a few seconds the whole scene in front of her seemed suffused with a faint green mist. Through this drifting mist Branwen caught glimpses of all the creatures of the forest. Around Cerridwen forest flowers seemed to be growing and bursting into bloom, and fronds of ivy seemed to creep over the old Druid's hands and arms. The very oaks around them seemed to be aware and alive in a new way that she had not seen before. Then, to her amazement, a beautiful roe buck appeared, walked straight up to Cerridwen, nudged her and then moved to Branwen, lying down and placing its antlered head on her lap. Just as suddenly, all these visions faded from view, and with a shaking voice Branwen told Cerridwen and Lorchar what she had seen. Cerridwen nodded and smiled her wide, friendly grin but her eyes were filled with tears.

'As I thought, it is all true then, all that Lord Myrthin and you, Lorchar thought about this young woman. Branwen, for forty years now I have lived in the forests and been beloved of Cerunnos the overlord spirit of the forest. I was his voice in the world of men, warning them to love the the forest and protect it. Reminding the people that they must respect the trees, the creatures, plants and spirits of the forest, whilst they use them. Although, for my age, I am still fit and healthy, I know that in the time to come, the time of the Romans, I cannot travel the land to remind our people what they owe to the spirits of the forest. For some time now, I have been praying that one would come, before the circle of my life is completed, that could replace me. Cerunnos assured me that one would come, to whom I could teach what I have learned. Now I know that he spoke truth, as he always does, and that person is you Branwen of Mona'

Branwen was shocked beyond all measure at these words from the kindly Cerridwen.

'But Lady Cerridwen, surely this person cannot be me. I am not fourteen until next month, and although I have certain unusual powers, in many ways I am still a silly little girl like others of my age. It is true that I do see things others do not see and had an experience recently that Lady Lorchar interpreted as Cerunnos showing me his favour. But how can I be ready to take on the mantle that you have worn for so long?'

'Your reluctance and modesty are most becoming, young lady' Cerridwen replied, with a fond smile, 'but what you saw in your vision just now was real and meaningful. You cannot yet communicate with Cerunnos directly, though I will show you how. When I took over this mantle, as you call it, I was not so many years older than you are now. At that age I did not have half the knowledge of the forests and of healing that you have. I have never mastered the art of disappearance as you have, and I never saw Cerunnos until the day he made his will known to me. What you saw just now is given to only one woman, always a woman, in every generation to see. Even the Lady Lorchar, for all her considerable powers will not have seen it, is that not so Lorchar?

A white faced Lorchar replied 'Indeed I saw nothing, though all my other senses were assailed. I could smell the flowers where there were none, hear the trees creak and the animals move, feel the very roots beneath the ground shift and sense in my heart and mind that something momentous was taking place, yet I saw nothing!'

Cerridwen rose from her seat on the ground and moved to Branwen. She took the girl's small hands in hers and lifted her to her feet. The old Druid put her hands to Branwen's brow and a garland of forest flowers appeared there. She embraced the shaking girl and a sense of utter calm descended upon her. A rush of rapid images of forest creatures and plants flashed across her minds eye and she felt a new sense of power and responsibility. The older woman spoke calmly and quietly to the young Druid.

'Branwen, all my powers you now share, you have much lore and technique to learn, and in the few days I have with you, I will do my utmost to pass on what I can. Remember that Lady Lorchar, although she is not favoured with your powers has great knowledge of the lore you will need, turn to her in the months ahead. But now, Branwen of Mona, favoured of Cerunnos, Lady of the Forests of Britain, do you accept your charge?'

Branwen swallowed hard, a few hours ago she had been a carefree young girl revelling in the great adventure she was caught up in and enjoying the growing powers she found she had. Now she was told, had seen and felt new powers and with them a huge responsibility she could barely imagine. However the powers passed to her by Cerridwen, powers she could feel but not yet understand, filled her with a new confidence.

'Lady Cerridwen, I accept my charge and pray that I will develop the skill and confidence to carry it out with the same devotion to Cerunnos and the spirits of the forest that you have shown for so long. Whatever the Romans do or say, nothing will stop me reminding the people of Britain what they owe to the Forest and how they should show their respect'

With these mature words the two women, old and young, embraced and were joined by Lorchar. All three shed copious tears and where they fell flowers appeared. At the edge of the glade a large roe buck stood and watched.

Chapter 10

The tall, slender Druid introduced as Cilmor stood up after Cerridwen had left the summit, and indicated to Cerna and Pered that they should follow him. The twins exchanged a glance, stood up and followed as this vigorous old man strode across the summit to a grassy area entirely surrounded by high rocks. Again, there was a fire already burning in the small, sheltered area. The old Druid stared intently at the twins, his dark eyes full of intelligence. The twins, not to be intimidated, stared back. What they saw was a man, probably in his early seventies, with very little hair on his head, but with a thick beard, the colour of iron. Beneath those intelligent, all seeing eyes was a prominent nose, like the beak of an eagle. Together these features gave him a rather fierce look, which was suddenly mitigated as he gave the young Bards a broad, warm smile. Then he spoke with a vibrant voice that was at once soothing yet insistent.

'Now, I have heard much about your skills and talents, but I could not be at the feast last night, so please excuse me if I judge these things for myself. Cerna, would you do me the honour of singing something for me?'

With this request made, Cilmor sat down while Cerna rose. She stared at the old Druid for a moment or two, then began to sing. In a low voice, as sweet as honey, Cerna sang of a land across the sea, a land of rocky headlands and green fields, a land of warm summers and wild, wet winters. A few minutes into her song she saw tears rolling down the cheeks of the fierce old man, and his eyes now seemed to be looking at a place far from this rocky hill. When her song was over the old Druid looked at Cerna with a new respect in his dark eyes.

'Girl, did someone tell you that I come from a land far from here, the land that the Romans call Armorica? Or did you divine it yourself by somehow seeing into my heart and mind?'

Cerna answered shyly, uncertain whether she had done the right thing.

'Lord Cilmor, I merely looked at you for a moment, and I saw images of a land I did not know, and a song I knew seemed to fit what I saw. I knew that what I sang would mean much to you, and I thought that you would want me to show what I can do, but I hope that I have not upset you in any way,'

'Cerna, you have exposed the raw edges of my very soul, for I love my homeland, and fear now that I will never see it again. But you did right. I now see that all I have been told about you is true. You are not just a Bard with a lovely voice. You have Druidic power, and a rare one, to see into men's souls and discover what will move them. Then the talent to use your exceptional voice to play on those emotions, like your brother plays his harp. In the task that lies ahead of all of you to keep the people of Britain aware of the Truth we tell, your skills will be invaluable. What I can teach you is how to use those skills, that voice, to sway a multitude.'

Cilmor turned now to Pered. 'Now young man, it seems you are a skilled story teller with a powerful voice. Is that the sum total of your talents I wonder? Let us see what you can do?

Stung by these remarks, Pered turned his pale, piercing eyes on Cilmor for a few moments, then took a deep breath and without warning, roared out the single word that began a famous old tale of war and courage. The word struck Cilmor like a physical blow, he took one step backwards placed his hand on his chest.

'I deserved that, for my my attitude and scepticism. I should have been more believing of what I have been told. But the simple fact is, that I have not come across one Druid or Bard capable of doing what you just did, for a generation, not since my old teacher died thirty years ago, in fact. For one so young to have so much power and direction in their voice is exceptional. I wonder if you even know what you did just then? You directed your voice precisely at me, and used its power and vibrations to shake up the very organs of my body. You must use that power with care Pered, for it could have killed a man of my age without my training. In the days available to me, I will show you how to use that power more accurately, to use against many, to use it to persuade, as well as strike, and I will teach you and your sister certain ancient words of power, known to very few, that can be used by voices such as yours, to command and even to destroy. I have used them in this way only twice in my life, and I urge you to be as sparing. It goes without saying that as Druids you should never use them for your own personal advantage, or they will lose their virtue and destroy you instead.'

Hearing these ominous words from the fierce old Druid caused the twins to look at each other white faced and shaking. No longer could they think of themselves merely as gifted entertainers, they began to be aware that they were young, but powerful Druids themselves, with a vital, but dangerous role to play in the future of their people.

Meanwhile, back at the summit of the hill, Alwyn sat under the close scrutiny of Old Huw and Machan the Druid from Erin who was placing a selection of strange herbs on the fire before them. It was Huw who spoke first.

'We need to begin, Alwyn by seeing something of what you can do. I would like you to look into Machan's mind. I know it is something you are reluctant to do in the normal way of things, but these are exceptional times, and there is much we must do that we find distasteful, as you have already discovered. Machan gives his full permission, and in truth there is little enough going on in that mind of his anyway.'

Machan gave a little laugh and his dark eyes twinkled as he nodded his assent to Alwyn. He spoke the common Btitish tongue, but with the lilt of a son of Erin

'Aye, and keep going lad, whatever little obstacles I may put in your way'

Alwyn focussed his mind on Machan's. Normally, on the few occasions he had done this, he had found it easy, but he was surprised to be met by what he could only describe as a wall preventing his entry. He tried to crash through the wall with the pure power of his mind, but though it rocked, there was no way through. Now he began probing the wall delicately, looking for weak points, when he found one, he eased it aside, and looked for more. Soon, he had breached enough of this mental wall to get beyond it. Almost immediately a kind of mist was everywhere, preventing him from seeing more. Alwyn had never encountered anything like this before, but his instinct was good, and he created in his mind, a kind of intense heat that seemed to burn the mist away. No sooner had he done this, when his mind was assailed by fearsome monsters of a sort he had never imagined. They seemed incredibly real, but Alwyn was made of sterner stuff. In his mind he conjured a great wind that blew them all away. Now he saw a young red headed boy on a rocky shore, waiting for a small boat to make its way across a reef of jagged rocks in a stormy sea. To his horror, he saw the small leather boat founder on the rocks, and and the people on board struggle and drown before his very eyes. The boy was on his knees at the edge of the sea screaming out for his father. He withdrew from Machan's mind, and saw the man himself on the other side of the fire with tears streaming down his wrinkled face. Machan looked up at him and gave a wry smile.

'That was the day I saw my father's fishing boat founder and watched him, my uncle and two brothers drown, sixty years ago. By the gods of Erin, I put enough barriers in your path to stop you seeing that, but in minutes you brushed them all aside. I only know of two people in all of Britain who could have done that. Huw here himself, and Maelgwyn who Huw taught before he went to the bad. You did this on on the power you were born with, and pure instinct. I have never seen the like'

'Machan is right' said Huw 'You have more innate potential than any other Druid I have ever heard of. If I had months to teach you, there is no limit to what you could achieve. But alas, we do not have months, so we must attempt a far riskier process. Because we both have the power to see into each other's minds, I believe I can pass all I know onto you, through a process that I have heard of, but never done. Machan has some special herbs that can help us achieve it, and he will supervise the process, which could be dangerous, if we were disturbed. We would join our minds together, and in perhaps as little as an hour, you would know all that I know. Learning to use that knowledge, I will have to leave your own intelligence and good sense. What do you say? Wait! you have until tomorrow to think about it. We have taken enough out of you today already I think, and your friends will soon return'

Owain and Garth returned to the hill fort physically exhausted by the day's exertions, but they were unprepared for the drawn grey faces of the other members of their party. The sheer emotional turmoil that the young Druids had gone through that day, as they began to understand the weight of expectation that lay across their youthful shoulders. They had also been shocked at the extent of the powers their mentors had revealed to them. Even Alwyn had not fully appreciated just what he might be capable of, and this revelation had had left him, let alone his less experienced fellows, shaking with the realisation that the future of their people's culture could well lay with them, if indeed the Romans were successful in their plan to eliminate Mona as the centre of Druidic learning and culture. None of them felt sure they were ready for the burden being placed on them by the powerful teachers they had worked with that day, however, all now knew that it was a burden they were bound to shoulder. Owain and Garth knew nothing of what had happened that day, but reading the shocked exhaustion in the faces of the younger members of the party, and seeing the narrow mouth and slight shake of the head made by Lorchar, Owain shook off his own tiredness and made a great deal of fuss about the food and drink prepared for them and told amusing tales of the day's battle training, always finding a story from his past to illustrate the tales. In this way the evening soon passed, and the younger Druids made their excuses for an early night, accompanied by Garth. Left alone for a while, Owain raised a quizzical eye at Lorchar, who shook her head as she recalled what she had seen and been told that day.

'Owain, even I had no idea what we were dealing with when we began this venture. I suppose that Myrthin knew, he always does, but I feel inadequately prepared for what I have seen and heard today. These ancient and skilled Druids have been simply amazed at the untapped talents these young people possess. Apparently, Alwyn may well turn out to be the most powerful Seer that we have ever had, Cerna and Pered turn out to have powers of the voice that it normally takes a lifetime for the adept to acquire, and what I have learned about Branwen I cannot even reveal to you, it is so sacred a secret. Suffice it say that the girl is very special indeed and I would not want to be the person, Roman or Briton who dared cross her. Owain, we knew what we did here was a vital task, else neither of us would have left Myrthin to do it, but only today have I fully realised why our beloved friend wanted us to undertake such a task. We have in our hands nothing less than the future of our culture. The Romans see it as a threat, and are intent on destroying it, by bringing down Mona, but I tell you this, as long as we keep these young people safe, and out of the hands of Maelgwyn or the Romans, we can face the future with confidence. The Romans may conquer our lands, may bring in their gods and stone cities, but whilst these young Druids live, our people will always know of the power of the Truth, and know that Rome has nothing to match it'

Owain sat dumbfounded by this speech. He had the greatest of respect for the intelligence and perception of the Pictish Druid and Princess, and what he had seen for himself in the past days had opened up his rather closed, prosaic mind to new possibilities. He stroked his grizzled jaw for a while before he replied.

'Lorchar, I am glad that what we do is as important as you say. In my mind I always felt that if Myrthin said it was vital, it must be so. I have seen things done these last few days, that I would not have believed possible before. Now you tell me that this is not even the half of what is possible. This puts a heavy burden of responsibility on us, but we must be aware that it places an even heavier burden on those young shoulders, as they begin to realise who, and what they are. We must try to make the rest of their quest as straightforward as possible, and do whatever we have to, in order to protect the precious talent we have as our wards. Now, though sleep may be difficult for both of us, we must try, for we have another arduous day tomorrow.'

Both went to their huts and eventually fell asleep dreaming of their old friend who had placed this burden upon them, knowing that he had been right to do so, and glad that they had agreed. They both shared a dream in which Myrthin smiled down upon them in their sleep and laid a reassuring hand upon their shoulders.

They were all awoken early the next morning, and after they had broken their fast, Alwyn took Owain aside with a worried look on his face.

'I hope by now that you have come to know that my talents usually warn me of dangers to me, and those I care for. Last night I dreamed very vividly of a threat to our well being. I believe that there is a traitor amongst those who you train in battle today. I cannot as yet tell who it is, or indeed if he is to be numbered amongst the king's men, or those of the prince. However, I do know that he is sworn to the Romans, and is planning to get news of us to a Roman spy. I believe he must have been specially trained by Maelgwyn, or he could not have put up such a strong barrier to my probing this morning. Perhaps you will know ways in which you can perceive falseness in one you combat.'

Owain looked thoughtfully at his young friend. 'Indeed, there are ways, but they are not certain. In your discussions with the old Druids today, it would be as well to think of a way of unmasking this traitor tonight, if Garth and I should fail, before he is able to do us too much damage. It would be hard for us from here on in, if the Romans knew of us, and the quest we are on. If Maelgwyn is working with them there may be no way of protecting our secret'

The Druids and warriors parted company as they had the day before. The Druids to the sacred hill and the warriors to the broad expanse of beach nearby, where they could practice their combat and battle tactics. Owain took Garth to one side and told him Alwyn's ill news.

'Garth we must meet each warrior in single combat today, and when we do so, we must look into each man's eyes in the way that I have taught you, and try to see truth or falsehood there. If this traitor is as well taught in the sly tricks of the spy, as Alwyn thinks he may be, we may fail in this, but at least we will know the measure of our adversary. I know the effort of this will be hard for me today, so I look to you to carry more than your fair share of the combats. Remember though, this man means harm to us and those we care for. We will do what we have to.'

Thankfully, the day was not as hot as the previous ones, but a strong wind blew off the sea and the footing was soft and tiring on the deep, soft sand of the beach. The men were given group exercises to perform, whilst Owain and Garth took each man aside to train them individually in how to combat Roman fighting techniques. In each combat, father or son would look carefully at the eyes of their opponent, watching for the telltale signs of a man living with falsehood. The day was a hard one, especially for the older man, and despite the coolness of the day, both were soon bathed in sweat. By the late afternoon all had received their individual tuition, and as the father and son threw cooling sea water over their heads, they took the opportunity to share a quiet word.

Garth spoke first. 'I spotted no one Father, how did your fare?'

Owain groaned as he straightened his back.'In truth, I grow too old for such exertions, but I also spotted no one. This spy has been taught by an expert, how to hide his thoughts from showing in his face, whether his teacher was his Roman master, or Maelgwyn himself. We must trust that the Druids, old and young have come up with a plan to unmask him'

Up on the Carn of the Spirits much of the day had indeed been spent in urgent discussion of how to find out this spy amongst them. Old Huw had taken it as a focus for the day's training of the young Druids, as well as bringing his own considerable knowledge and cunning to bear on the problem. Lorchar was pleased that she too had been able to make a useful contribution to the emerging plan. Before the day was ended Huw and Machan took Alwyn to one side. Huw spoke first. 'Well my boy, I hope that amongst all else, you have had time to consider my proposal of last night. Will you take the risk of learning much of what I know through a meeting of our minds under the influence of Machan' special tincture?'

Alwyn took a deep breath and spoke up. 'It seems to me that, given what we now know, I must take the risk. What we have proposed for tonight may well work anyway, but with the additional power and knowledge this might provide, we have a better chance of success.'

Machan clapped Alwyn on the shoulder and spoke 'Bravely said, Alwyn. Now sit here and drain this cup in one draft. You will feel strange very quickly, and then you will pass from normal awareness, to a different state. You will be aware of far more, and in that state Huw will attempt to enter your mind, and I can only say pour his knowledge and power into you. On no account resist, as that could endanger both of you.'

With these ominous words Machan passed Alwyn a golden cup with a foul smelling concoction in it. Alwyn drained the cup and shook his head. Immediately, whilst his head swam, he was sharply aware of the voices of his comrades many hundreds of yards away, of the smell of pine trees a mile away, and of colours more vivid than he had ever seen before. He was enjoying this experience when he felt the sensation of someone trying to penetrate his mind. It was hard not to resist, as his only previous experience was of the intrusions of Maelgwyn. Somehow he found the strength to let it happen, and the experience grew immediately more astonishing. Pictures, words, ideas, thoughts, simply flooded his mind in a way that was so overwhelming that he almost passed out. Only Machan's calm voice, and his firm grip on the young Druid's arm kept him conscious. It was Huw's voice that eventually broke the trance

'Well my boy, now you know all that I know. though you will not yet know fully how to use it. I have glimpsed into your mind tonight and I know that you, along with your friends can indeed achieve what Myrthin hoped, and keep the spirit and knowledge of the Truth, and our culture alive at least for one more generation. But we have an urgent task to accomplish tonight, so for now, catch up your fellows and we will all meet at the king's hall tonight. But wait, I forget one important matter. You have had the good taste not to mention a great treasure of our people that you wish to take away from us. I refer, of course to the Torc of Aneurin. No boy, do not protest, I know Myrthin's reasons for this task better than you. We the Court Druids of the Demetae have kept this treasure safe for generations until one

one would come with the power to wield it in the cause of the Truth. You are that chosen one and tonight you will wear it and feel its power.'

Alwyn set off swiftly after the others. Outwardly, he was the same, but inside he knew all had changed. He was still the same Alwyn but a new strength and confidence flowed through his veins, he knew things he had not known a short while before, and he was sure that there was little he could not accomplish, if he set his mind to it. He suspected he would need all his new found power and knowledge to achieve what he would have to do this evening.

That evening, warriors and Druids alike were enjoying the king's hospitality, when Owain and Huw stood up together. Owain banged his drinking cup hard on the table and bellowed in his parade ground voice for silence. Huw looked round the room for a few moments before he spoke.

'This is a hard thing for me to say, as I know all present here, and their families for two generations at least. However, say it I must. Amongst us here tonight, eating the king's food and drinking his mead, sharing jokes with comrades, is a traitor, a man who has sold his sword to the Romans, and to their ally, that snake Maelgwyn. Tonight we must unmask him and kill him'

Amongst the hubbub of raised voices that these revelations caused, the voices of the king and the prince rose above all. Despite their differences, the prince fell silent to allow his father to speak first.

'In truth, I can scarce believe these words, but I have come to trust what Huw has told me over many years, and we know that we have young Druids amongst us, with powers we can scarcely guess at. I will say this though, if there is a traitor here at my own hearth, bent on doing harm to our honoured guests, though I know you all, and count you as friends as well as subjects, I myself will strike off his head with my own sword tonight, before you all!'

It was now the prince' s turn to speak, and in a voice shaking with emotion, he shouted out his words. 'Each one of the men I brought here last night was chosen by me for their bravery and hatred of the Romans, so I cannot believe that a traitor hides amongst them, but if there is, let him speak now, and I will fight him in single combat to expiate my shame. In that way, he will at least die with the honour of holding his sword in his hand, even if all other honour is dead to him. If not, and he is found out, I will place my hand on the hilt of my father's sword as he strikes off that man's head'

Not to be outdone, Lydd as the king's champion repeated the offer of single combat if the traitor should be one of the king's warriors. No one spoke and no one moved. After a moment or two, Huw called on Alwyn to speak.

'You do not know me very well as yet, and you may have reason to doubt the powers of one as young as me. Very well, if you do, speak to Huw here, who you know to be great Druid. He will tell you what I can do. Know this, however, what is about to happen will be a frightening spectacle, that many of you will tell your grandchildren of, but if you are still for the Truth, you have nothing to fear. One here present has a great deal to fear, before king or prince strike off his head, he will know a thousand torments, that the rest of you will never experience. So do not rely on what you have been taught by Maelgwyn, it will not avail you here, but speak now, and die that warrior's death you have been promised, or die a death that you will soon pray to come, from to the gods and spirits you have deserted'

With these ominous words ringing in the years of the silent men, Alwyn stalked out of the hall. As he left, the tall stately figures of Cerna and Pered entered, dressed in the white state robes of senior bards. As they entered, Cerna began singing in a high, keening voice that set the warriors' nerves jangling. She was singing in an ancient, unknown tongue, but somehow it played on all the emotions of the gathered throng. Soon men were crying, shaking with fear, sobbing with a sense of loss. Some even lost control of their bladders. Then Pered's powerful bass joined the song. His voice seemed to shake their internal organs, made their brains rattle against their skulls. Now men were retching, holding their heads, passing out. Suddenly the singing stopped and Pered's mighty voice rang out words which they could understand, but which filled them with even greater dread.

'Men of the Demetae, you are greatly honoured, for tonight you meet one that few mortals ever see, and live to tell the tale. Blodauwedd, The Lady of Flowers, Queen of the Forest, Beloved of Cerrunnos, will pass amongst you, with her familiar the Spirit of The Wolf. Only one man here tonight has anything to fear, though what you see will fill you all with dread'

Pered stepped back and from a greenish mist that had appeared from nowhere, was Branwen, but unlike the Branwen any of them had seen before. She seemed to float in the unearthly mist, in a long, flowing gown of the finest green material. In her long hair were flowers in abundance, and the scent of forest flowers filled the room with a heady aroma. As flowers fell from her hair more appeared and the path she had taken was strewn with flowers. At her heels stalked a huge grey she wolf, with slavering jaws and a reddish light in its eyes. Branwen walked amongst the men, looking each one in the face. Some could not face her, and she gently raised the head of each that turned away, and stared into their eyes. A light of green and gold shone from Branwen's eyes, which at first calmed the men, until they watched the flowers in her hair unfurl and turn to serpents before their eyes. If any tried to move away, they found the wolf spirit barring their way with an angry snarl. Then, as swiftly as she had appeared, she left the hall. Now Alwyn was back, with the old Druids behind him. The rest were all wearing the grey robes of the Mona trained Druid. Alwyn though, was all in black, a rare colour reserved for the most senior of Druids. Round his neck was a heavy torc of gold, and round his head a thin circlet of gleaming bronze. In his hand, a great black staff tipped with gold. Alwyn crashed the staff down on the wooden boards of the king's raised dais, and silence fell on the assembled warriors, who were now deeply in awe of the young Druids.

Slowly, but inexorably, the warriors felt the strange and frightening sensation of of someone, or something, entering their minds. It was a physical sensation, like slender tendrils creeping through the passageways of their brain. Images from their past would flash briefly in their mind's eye, before fading away. For some the experience was too much, and they fainted dead away. Most felt uncomfortable, but felt that they had nothing to fear. One man though, was in abject terror as he realised that the protection given to him by Maelgwyn was no good any more. His eyes were wide, and the sweat was pouring from his face. He longed to pull his dagger, and make a break for it, but he was unable to move a muscle. He looked at the young Druid and the gold Torc around Alwyn's neck seemed to be pulsating with power and indeed he felt a heavy weight around his own neck, tightening and making breathing difficult.

Alwyn crashed down his staff once more and broke the spell of silence, but the sense of awe kept all the men quiet, especially when they saw, in front of Alwyn the mighty frames of Owain and Garth in full armour burnished to a bright shine. Owain had his long Gaulish sword drawn and Garth was hefting his huge double headed axe. Alwyn stretched out his slim arm and sealed the fate of the Demetae's traitor.

'The warrior named Gwalch step forward, for all should know that he is the traitor that would sell our secrets to the Romans, and destroy what remains of our culture and beliefs. Step forward and face your fate!'

In truth he did not need to step forward to identify himself, as all those around him stepped away from him, as though he was the source of a deadly plague. King Maelor's face was black with fury as he gripped the hilt of his sword and looked at his son, the Prince, whose sworn man Gwalch was. Prince Daelor's face was a mix of anger and sorrow as he watched Owain and Garth drag a tall, slim young warrior with a black beard up to the King's dais. King Maelor, normally the calmest of men could barely contain his anger as he spoke.

'Gwalch Ap Teilo, is this true? Have you brought shame on the memory of your honoured father, your family, your village, on me, and on my son, who I know, thought highly of you?'

The young man, although white with fear, summoned up enough spirit to answer, 'Lord King, that is not the way I see it. I was long ago convinced that the Romans were going to take over all of our lands anyway, and that their victory would be good for us all. No more wars with the Silures and Ordovices, and even the raiders from Erin would think twice, once we were under Roman protection. As you know, a few years ago, I travelled to the land of the Atrebates, and I was mightily impressed with with the life their people led, compared to ours. One day I fell into discussion with a distinguished man who turned out to be Lord Maelgwyn, and a Roman, who I later discovered to be one of their chief spies, a man I knew only as Marcus. We had several meetings, and they persuaded me that the best thing I could do for my people was to return and pretend to foment anti Roman feeling, in that way flushing out those who hated Rome. Lord Maelgwyn promised me that he would use his powers to protect me from discovery. Prince Daelor, I am sorry that I betrayed you, for you showed me great favour, but you must see that I believed I was doing all for the good of our people'

Daelor could no longer contain his fury and rushed at Gwalch, dagger in hand and would have surely finished the matter there if Garth had not grabbed his wrist.

'You snake! your apology is worth nothing, it was you who finally persuaded me that the only way to get our people to fight the Romans, was to gather those who believed as I did, to break away from my father, causing us both great sorrow, when all along you were giving our names to this spy, and no doubt planning that when the Romans defeated us you would be the one given the leadership of the Demetae. Father, I beg you, give me your sword and let me the one who strikes off the head of this traitor, who has caused so much bad feeling between us!'

The King, now calmer and with tears in his eyes at these signs of reconciliation with his son, spoke in a more measured way 'My son I am minded to accede to your request, but first we must know how much of the recent information, about our young friends here has been passed to this Marcus and to that other traitor, Maelgwyn?'

Gwalch, with a bitter laugh, replied 'In a very real sense Maelgwyn knows whatever I know, only this display of power from these young Druids today, broke the control he he had over my mind. As to Marcus, he showed me how to pass messages out of here to him, and within a day or two he will know of these Druids' presence amongst us. So, soon, these displays of Druidic magic will be fit only for shows to impress children. The Romans will have broken the power of Mona and Marcus or Maelgwyn will have these last remnants of that power in their control!'

'So it seems there is no repenting of your sins Gwalch. Prince Daelor, here is my sword. Do what you must do. It is small enough punishment for the enormity of the man's crimes'

With these words King Maelor handed his son his great sword. Owain, Garth and Lydd forced the struggling Gwalch to lay his head over a bench, and with one mighty blow Daelor struck the traitor's head from his body. In the whole assembled throng only Cerna turned away her head.

King Maelor called Owain, Garth, Lorchar, Huw, Lydd, Daelor and the young Druids to meet him in his private quarters. His emotions were a mixture of embarrassment that his guests should have been put to such exertions on his behalf, and fury at Maelgwyn for creating a spy and traitor in his court. As a good host he knew his first responsibilities.

'Lord Owain, Lady Lorchar, I am ashamed that this should have happened whilst you and your charges were staying with us, and I know that my son shares my shame and anger. However, we must be realistic, what has happened tonight was witnessed by many and will spread like wildfire across my lands and that of my neighbours. The Romans were already interested, and they will surely learn quickly of the amazing turn of events here this evening. My first responsibility is to you. I hear from Huw that your next destination is a to an old friend of his on Ynys Avalon. Well it so happens I have a ship in the bay near here, laden with goods to trade with our good friends and cousins the Dubonii, in whose lands the island lies. Tomorrow, at dawn you will be on that ship. The land of the Dubonii is riddled with Romans, but they are a cunning folk, used to hiding much from their overbearing new friends. You will be taken to a river on the south side of the Havren Sea. From there you will be supplied with ponies and a guide, for finding the way to Ynys Avalon is fraught with dangers. I wish you good luck, though with the powers of your young friends, I doubt you will need it. I do not forget what damage Maelgwyn has done to me and my son and soon he will pay for it. Daelor my boy, you and Lydd will pick seventy men and tomorrow set off for Maelgwyn's lair and destroy it. Huw will do what he can to hide our intentions, but it may be that the sly fox will escape the hunt again. So be it, he will have no lair to return to and no men to fight his battles from here on. Let my will be done!'

So it was that early the next morning the young Druids and their protectors found themselves on board a small ship laid up in the river that led out past the dunes to the open sea. Straying never far from the rocky coast, the ship sailed south and anchored that night in a huge sheltered haven at the entrance to the Havren Sea. The next day they sailed East, past cliffs and sandy bays before anchoring in a shallow, muddy estuary. On the third day, they could see the south side of the Havren Sea, the land of Dubonii, and late in the day pulled into a river estuary in that land, where as promised ponies and a thin and silent man who was their guide waited for them. By now, Owain did not even pause to wonder how the orders of King Maelor could travel faster than his swiftest ship.

Meanwhile, far to the north, Maelgwyn was a worried man. He confided his fears to Bran. 'I can learn nothing from King Maelor's land. I did not think Old Huw capable of blocking me in this way, he must have learned something from the boy. However, one thing is certain, the King will seek revenge. Since we cannot tell when that will happen, you and I will flee. On our own we can slip away unseen by Ordovices and Romans alike. I will go to a place I long ago prepared for this eventuality. I want you to go to Marcus and keep him focused on the boy, as there will be much else to distract him in the weeks to come. He must continue to believe that he needs that boy and his fellows to secure his own future'

Bran blanched, his already white face drained of any remaining colour as he realised he was about to lose his comfortable home, the cheery young woman who shared it with him and all that could not be carried away on horseback. As always, Maelgwyn saw his thoughts as they flashed through his mind unbidden.

'Do not even think of warning that woman of yours, that you have become so fond of. We must be gone within the hour and no one must know of our leaving. If I were you, I would kill the woman. It would be a kindness, if that young wolf Daelor falls upon our little fold.'

So it was that in the early dawn, two horsemen slipped away from the hidden little valley, one seeing only a setback in his larger plans, the other using all the techniques he had learned over years to hide his sorrow and rage over the terrible 'kindness' he had just performed.

An hour later seventy furious warriors swept into the valley, without opposition since the sentries had been killed by Maelgwyn and Bran. The twenty or so remaining warriors of Maelgwyn's band were swiftly dispatched and the women and children bound and taken into slavery, worse fates having been spared them by the towering figure and baleful eyes of Lydd. The victory had been easy, with no men lost from the attacking force and only a few slight wounds to deal with. However, Daelor did not look happy.

'So, the old fox has escaped the justice he deserves and left his people to pay the price of his crimes.' He growled to a grim looking Lydd. The older man replied.

'Yes, old Huw must have succeeded in shielding our approach from Maelgwyn's mind, but the man has other powers and may have felt attack was inevitable. Doubtless he had his own reasons for running away with only that black crow Bran as companion. In the end I believe that only Alwyn and his friends will have the power to deal with Maelgwyn. I think he has over reached himself in trying to destroy those young Druids, for they will become much more powerful than him and will not forget all he has done to try and destroy them, and all they believe in.'

The hotheaded young prince spat as he cleaned the blood from his sword. 'You may be right Lydd, but I would have loved the chance to see if his magic could turn my blade away as I swung at his head!'

Chapter 11

Back in the south, Owain and the others were becoming grateful for the presence of their taciturn guide. After a morning's ride through gentle hills filled with livestock, the travellers had emerged into flat lands, marshes and water meadows that gave way to shallow lakes at a moment's notice. Their ponies travelled single file along narrow paths shielded by tall reeds, or along old wooden walkways, too slippery to ride along, they had to dismount and walk. Periodically gaunt men with ragged clothes would appear, spear in hand from amongst the reeds and stare blankly at them as they passed by. Without their guide they would have had no way to find the correct path through this watery landscape. In the distance they could see the steep rounded hill rise impossibly from the flat surrounding land. This was the famed Tor, the sacred hill where the feared White Druid of Ynys Avalon communed with the spirit world.

When they finally reached Ynys Avalon they found a gentle, favoured land, a land that seemed rich and contented. Soon, some figures approached on horseback. They were led by a tall young man with long golden hair. Just behind him, on a white horse, rode a woman, tall as the young lord, dressed entirely in white and with waist length, pure white hair held back from her face by the bronze band of a Druid. Behind them rode a band of warriors carrying spears, but no swords. The golden haired young man rode forward and raised his right hand in greeting.

'Welcome to Ynys Avalon. My name in Prince Tai, I am the younger son of King Maldwyn of the Dubonii and I serve him as Lord of Avalon. We knew of your coming because of the skills and power of the Lady Eirlys, our chief Druid and known across the Island of Britain as the White Druid of Avalon, may I present her to you?'

At these words the tall Druid rode forward and smiled as she looked at each of the travellers. Despite her white hair, she was a lady in her forties, with the palest of blue eyes, and a look of sharp intelligence which her broad smiles could not hide. Looking at each of them in turn, she welcomed each by name.

'Lord Owain, your skills as a warrior are renowned across Britain, I knew your late wife well and it is a joy to see what a fine young man your son, Garth has grown to become. Lady Lorchar, I know with what regard Lord Myrthin holds you, and that should be enough for anyone to know your worth. Lord Alwyn, Old Huw has passed to me information on your powers, and also on your qualities as a man and Druid, and now I can see in you, that he spoke the truth. We are honoured to have you here. Lady Branwen, never has Avalon welcomed one who holds the honour granted to you recently, I hope you will sanctify our famous oak grove with your presence. Lord Pered and Lady Cerna, we have heard much of your outstanding talents and hope that you will agree to share a little of them with us this evening. Garth, I see much of your mother in you, and I hope that while you are here, you will allow me to discover how much of your mother's talents you share'

All but one seemed happy with Eirlys' words. Alwyn, Branwen, Pered and Cerna were flattered at being addressed with the honorific Lord and Lady, normally only accorded to very senior Druids and Bards, especially as they had been so honoured by such a well respected Druid as Eirlys. Lorchar was pleased with the reference to Myrthin and Garth was delighted to meet someone who knew his mother, as Owain so rarely talked of her. Owain, however was not pleased. Much as he had loved Garth's mother, there were aspects of that lady's life that he did not wish Garth to know about. The displeasure must have shown on Owain's face, and Eirlys seemed troubled by it. As they rode towards the heart of Avalon, the Druid took the opportunity to ride alongside Owain and talk to him privately.

'Lord Owain, I am sorry if you were unhappy with my words of welcome. I was under the impression that you and the boy's mother were much in love, and therefore that you would appreciate it, if I could see aspects of her in your fine son'

Owain, sorry now that he had let his feelings show in such a crass way was moved to explain himself. 'I am sorry Lady Eirlys, I would never wish to offend you, least of all because you knew and liked my beloved late wife. However, I have never hidden my dislike of some of the trappings of the Druidical hierarchy, despite my love of my wife, and of my old friend Myrthin. Of late, I have grown very fond of Lady Lorchar and my young charges, but you must know that I have never told Garth that his mother was a Druid of some power. I have never wanted him to even think of moving in that direction, and have never seen any inclination on his part towards the life my wife lived before she met me'

The White Druid of Avalon smiled gently at the grizzled old warrior, before replying. 'Owain, by now you must understand the battle for the future of our beliefs and culture, that we are in the midst of. You will have seen what these exceptional young people are capable of, and how important they are for our future. Well, I believe I have seen something special in Garth, a portion of what his mother was. Would you deny your son the chance to be all that he can be? Would you deny him full knowledge of what his mother was? I see a great sadness in him. It is hard enough to lose your mother at such a tender age, it is worse to be denied full knowledge of her. However painful it may be for you, you should reconsider your position on this matter. Your son is already a great warrior in the making, but he can be even more if you will allow it'

A long silence followed, but Owain knew that the Druid was right, he had been wrong to hide so much of his mother's past from his son. He would have to find the time now to put right that wrong. However that would have wait a little while longer, as they were now entering Avalon's main village. There were two large round houses in the village, one belonging to prince Tai and the other to Eirlys. In the prince's house, a large table was set for a meal. Before that, the female guests were taken to Eirlys's house to refresh themselves, whilst the men were offered the same opportunity at the home of the prince.

Meanwhile, three days journey to the north, in a nondescript home in a Roman military town, a stocky middle aged man who might have been a retired soldier, or perhaps a merchant who had not been as successful as he might have been, stalked the main living room of the house angrily.

'What do mean, you don't know what has happened there? I pay you to know. I paid for a man to be trained in these crazy Druidical mind tricks, so that no one could guess he was a spy. Now you tell me that one day after he gets a message to you that these young Druids with great powers have arrived for training by King Maelor's chief Druid, my spy just disappears, and that furthermore, these young Druids and their protectors are no longer there, and no one will, or can, tell you where they are gone. I am a Roman, this magic nonsense means nothing to me. I am prepared to believe the turncoat Maelgwyn, if he tells me that this boy he talks of, has special mental powers, that the Governor, or even the Emperor might be willing to pay well for, but I do not believe that the whole party of them can disappear into thin air!'

The thin, poorly dressed Briton in front of him shrugged. 'All I can do, Marcus, is keep my ear to the ground. This party of young Druids and a Pictish princess Druid accompanied by two large, well armed warriors, wherever they appear, will not be missed, and in due course we will hear of it. In the meantime, I do have some news for you. Bran, Maelgwyn's right hand man has been seen, travelling alone through the mountains, just west of here. He should be here by tomorrow.'

Marcus, calmer by now, stroked his clean shaven chin thoughtfully 'It must be an important matter if Maelgwyn is prepared to spare Bran to travel alone through the wild lands of the Silures. Bran is too well known, and too distinctive in appearance. Take some men and ride out on the western approaches. Meet Bran and bring him to me in disguise. Not here, but to that little inn that I use in the south of the town. With Maelgwyn's skills at his disposal, Bran may be able to help us find these Druids even sooner'

To the South, the young Druids, Lorchar, Owain and Garth all took their places at a feast in their honour in Prince Tai's hall. They told the tale of their remarkable journey so far, to the great approval of all those present. Eirlys and Lorchar, however looked more worried, and exchanged anxious words as the tale of the journey was unfolding. Eirlys leaned across to Owain, to share their concerns.

'Lord Owain, you and your charges are vital to the future of our people and culture, and you have certainly deserved all the honour Prince Tai has done you here tonight, but now you are in territory that is deeply influenced and infiltrated, if not yet completely controlled by the Romans. Many here are afraid of of upsetting them, after all there are garrisons a day's march from here. Many more, sad to relate have been infected by the Roman love of money. It will be hard to keep your presence here a secret. It is certain that the Romans would not wish your mission to succeed, so we may not have much time to do what Myrthin charged me to do some months ago. So I must ask if we can make an early start tomorrow. I will need everyone except you, to accompany me to the Tor at sunrise tomorrow.'

The sadness in Owain's eyes was all too obvious to Eirlys. 'Yes Owain, even Garth. I can see that there is something in him that has come from his Mother. A power that we must harness. If we do not Owain, it may be, that in extremity, that power will emerge in a way that cannot be controlled, and then you could lose him forever. He needs to recognise it, learn to control it and use it to serve the Truth. This does not mean that he will have to follow the path of the Druid. Indeed it does not strike me that he is deeply spiritual. However this part of him that he has inherited from his mother is too powerful to ignore, so Garth must come too. Perhaps tonight, you should speak to him about his mother.'

Soon the feast ended and the Druids were told to prepare for an early start the following day. As they walked to their beds, Owain took Garth's arm and led him aside.

'Son I need to talk to you tonight. Tomorrow, you must accompany the Druids to the Tor. Eirlys wants to include you in her work. As she hinted earlier today, this has to do with your mother. I know you do not remember much about her, though you memory of her is fond. What you do not know, is that she was a Druid. She came from the high mountains of Eryri. She was brought to Mona by Myrthin, because of her powers. Anyway, we met and although I was so much older than her, somehow we fell in love. When we talked about marriage, I told her that my views about religion meant that I could not marry a practising Druid, and she gave it all up for me. She died when you were a young child, as you know. To my shame, I kept from you the truth about about what she was, because I did not want you to follow that path, and Myrthin, out of respect for me helped me keep that secret. However, the lady Eirlys has told me that she can see that you have within you some of your mother's powers, and she has convinced me that you must learn what they are and how to control them, else one day they may appear in a time of danger and destroy you. I now know that I was wrong to to hold on to my prejudices about the Druids. Of course I have seen at first hand the powers our friends have, and I have accepted that it is for the good of us all on the Island of Britain to stay in touch with the Truth. You go with Eirlys tomorrow with my blessing, and what you do with the powers you discover is your choice. I know that you will always do the right thing.' The two massive warriors embraced and both were sobbing.

Just as the sun rose the following morning the Druids were woken by Eirlys's assistants, and after a light breakfast were taken to the Tor. Eirlys was waiting for them at the top of the Tor, next to a strange, low building with no windows, and made of stone and turf. Eirlys pointed to the building and told them of its purpose.

'This is a sweat house, it is one of the things the first Druids in Britain learned from the shamen of the ancestor folk. This one is now the last one in the south of Britain. One of very few left in the whole island. In it a fire is lit, and the smoke let out. It gets very hot and with some special herbs and drugs, those inside can soon enter a trance state, which will enable them to access areas of the spirit not normally available to them. We will all make use of it today and many of you will see things which may seem frightening at first, but nothing in there can harm you. Lorcha and I will be there to help and reassure you. You will all need to remove your clothes and wrap one of these plaid blankets round you, though after a short while even that may seem too much. Do not be shy, naked we entered this world and sometimes closeness to the spirit world requires the absence of clothes'

With this, Eirlys stepped out of her loose fitting white robe and wrapped a blanket round her lean white body. Lorcha and a laughing Branwen followed suit and more reluctantly, with much turning and holding of clothes, the others did the same, and followed Eirlys through the low, narrow entrance. Inside, the heat hit them like a blow, there was no smoke but water scented with herbs was thrown on hot stones, and a powerful, though pleasant smell was infused into the steam. Eirlys gave each of the young Druids and Garth a wad of herbs to chew on. The herbs did not taste so bad, but they soon took effect and, along with the steamy heat, all in the hut soon felt relaxed and slightly detached. Soon, the plaid blankets were abandoned and each person seemed to focus on their own breathing and took little notice of the others. All except Eirlys, who was watching each of the young people very carefully. First to fall into a full trance was Branwen.

Branwen saw, through a green mist, the glades of her beloved forest. She could smell the forest flowers and could hear and see even the smallest creatures in that forest. At the edge of the glade she could see the large Roe buck that she now recognised as the manifestation of Cerrunnos. In front of him were a number of creatures, sitting perfectly still. There was the wildcat, the creature to which Branwen felt the greatest affinity. In addition was a weasel, lithe and sharp, a white owl, sharp eyed and restless and finally there was a hare, sacred to the Druids. Branwen did not know what to make of this vision, and soon she drifted off into a deep sleep.

Pered was the next one to see something. Again the vision began in the forest. This part of the forest was dense with trees and undergrowth, then he saw the great forest hawk, silently, and at seemingly impossible speed, fly through this apparently impenetrable forest. Without warning, the vision changed, from one where he was watching the hawk, to one where he appeared to be seeing things through the eyes of the hawk as it headed towards non existent gaps, and changed direction, and tucked in wings at the the last moment, negotiating the forest at speeds that seemed impossible.

Pered felt an inexpressible exhilaration at the vision. It was not just the speed and stunning agility of the bird. In a sense he was not watching it, he was experiencing it. It made Pered feel like he was at last part of something he was made for, something that had been missing from his life. After what seemed like a few minutes, Pered felt a deep physical exhaustion. He wanted to continue this experience but was unable to do so. Inexorably he fell into a sleep that was more like unconsciousness.

Garth had entered the sweat house with no expectations of seeing, or experiencing anything. His father's matter of fact approach to life, and antipathy to religion had imbued in him the same scepticism, though events of past weeks had done something to change that. He knew the others had special powers, but despite the revelation about his mother, he had never had any inclination that there was anything different about him, other than his extraordinary skills as a warrior. He had watched, as first Branwen, and then Pered seemed to drift off into some fascinating world of their own, their pupils dilating and smiles wreathing their faces. He could see the concentration of the others, as they could clearly follow what was happening, but he saw nothing. Until that is, he saw his mother. He had always kept an image of his mother in his mind, young though he was when she died, but in truth, as time had gone on that image grew less clear. Yet here, in his mind's eye, was an image of her, clearer than any he could remember. And now his mother was speaking to him, speaking in that gentle, loving way he could just about remember, telling him not to be afraid, that he was about to learn something of the other part of her life, as a Druid. Something that she was now able, from the spirit world, to pass on to him. The image faded and was replaced by another. This time he could see a high, wild place of rocky knolls and sparse, stunted trees, the high mountains of his mother's youth perhaps. Then, from a narrow fissure in the rocks emerged a bear, clearly a she bear because behind her emerged a small cub. The mother bear raised her muzzle into the mountain air, and smelled something she did not like, her lip curled back and a low grumbling growl came from her great neck as she rose up on her hind legs. Then Garth saw the reason for her distress, a pack of five hungry wolves were circling the mother and cub. The she bear pushed her young cub back into the den, and then she stood four square in front of it, growling and showing her array of fearsome teeth. The wolves must have been very hungry, to risk their lives, but on they came, darting in, and snapping at the bear, who lashed out with her powerful forepaws, and snapped with massive jaws. One by one, she killed the wolves, at some cost to herself, as she bled from numerous savage bites. In the end she was victorious, and retreated to her lair to lick her wounds and suckle the young cub she had defended so heroically. At this point the image faded, to be replaced by another one of a young, powerful male bear emerging from that same lair. This bear swung his head around in the way bears do when sampling the scents in the air, then moved off into a patch of forest only to emerge in a furious charge on a pack of of wolves. The wolves fought fiercely but were no match for the speed and power of the bear who killed them all before filling the air with a powerful roar. Again the image faded and Garth too fell into a deep sleep.

Eirlys, Lorchar, Alwyn and Cerna sat up and looked around at the sleeping bodies of their three companions. It was Eirlys, who spoke first. 'We will leave these three here to sleep after what they have seen. There is a spring nearby where we can wash off the sweat of this place and discuss what we have seen today.'

She led them to a pool constantly fed by a bubbling spring. She discarded her blanket and entered the pool. She was followed by Lorchar and then rather more bashfully by Alwyn and Cerna. The coolness of the spring water felt good and they all tingled with its chill on heat reddened skin. Lorchar was the next to speak.

'I think Branwen's vision was clear, there are, as she thought, other creatures that she can take the spirit of, if she wishes, and with Cerrunnos' blessing. I am guessing that Pered has an affinity with the spirit of the Goshawk and will be able to learn how to make use of that now. However, I confess that Garth's vision puzzled me more. I admit I am not as accomplished a seer as you three, so there may well be aspects of it that I missed, and I must confess that the picture of the wolves in his vision was upsetting to me, as one with affinity to the spirit of the wolf.'

Eirlys laughed 'You must not take it personally, Lorchar, real wolves must eat, and there's no morality in their need to kill to eat. No, that was a message to Garth from his mother in the world of the spirits. She was a Druid as you know, she was also one of the very last people in this land to have affinity with the spirit of the bear. Real bears are almost gone from our land now and the spirit of the bear has grown weaker with its scarcity. But Garth's mother had that spirit powerfully, and could transform herself into the spirit of the bear at will. Since her death the spirit of the bear has been absent from our island. But now the spirit has been passed to Garth. I do not think that he will be able to fully transform, but when the need arises he will be able to incorporate that spirit, and the strength, speed and ferocity it brings, into himself. He will not appear as the bear, but will have its attributes.'

Alwyn, who had been silent and thoughtful until now, spoke up. 'Something is nagging away at me and I do not yet know what it is, but I have a presentiment that in the time to come, all of our companions and indeed the rest of us will have need of these powers revealed today. Will our friends know of these powers when they wake, or will you have to interpret their visions for them Lady Eirlys?'

The White Druid thought for a moment before replying. 'You must realise that this is a relatively new experience for me. I was taught the lore and method of this a lifetime ago, but until now have had no opportunity to fully put it into practice. The skill of transformation and linking with a spirit is rare indeed. So to have three at one time is more than I could ever have forseen. However, I do believe that Branwen who has, I understand, performed transformation already will have a good understanding of the significance of what she has seen. Pered is new to this but his upbringing and character will have given him some belief in his own specialness and I think he has a closeness to the great forest hawk in his way of being. So it will seem strange but, he will, I think, be anxious to try his his new skills out. As for Garth, we must all look after him now, he would have had no idea about this, with his not knowing of his mother's true nature. So, even if he has, as the old Druids say 'dreamed the bear' he will not have understood its significance. He will be bewildered and upset by today's revelations, I am sure.'

Soon the other three emerged, bleary eyed and shaking their heads as they pondered their visions. They found the rest of the party still enjoying the cool of the spring after the sultry heat of the sweat house. Branwen, free of inhibitions as always, threw off her blanket with a laugh and lowered herself into the cooling pool. Pered, more reticent, but proud of his status as a Druid, shrugged and slipping off the blanket moved with grace and speed into the spring. Garth, shy of these experiences, but bewildered and keen to find out more from Eirlys, rather clumsily tried to climb into the pool and free himself of the clinging woolen blanket at the same time, causing much amusement as he managed to drag the whole blanket into the cold water. Everyone's laughter broke the ice of any awkwardness about the situation and soon everyone was talking excitedly about the visions and what they meant. Eirlys managed to explain to Garth what his vision really meant though he could scarcely believe it. He was still upset about not knowing until now, such an important fact about his mother. Cerna, intensely aware of the feelings of others as always, wanted to move closer to comfort him but she became acutely aware of their nakedness, and could not see how to bring comfort without creating embarrassment. Instead, she closed her eyes and conveyed her sympathy and care to Garth through the young man's mind. Garth understood what was happening and why and gave his beautiful friend a shy smile.

When, in due course, they had all cooled down and emerged from the pool pulling on their clothes, they made their way back down to the village. Most of them still talking excitedly about the day's events. Alwyn, however, remained rather silent as he tried to bring some clarity to the vague presentiment he had experienced earlier. Cerna tried to help him but found her mind could not follow where Alwyn led. Branwen too, noticed Alwyn's silence and worried frown. She drew up to him and shyly gave his arm a squeeze, and even in his preoccupied state, Alwyn could not help but give a smile of gratitude to the ebullient girl Druid. Eirlys too, noticed Alwyn's worry, and whispered to him that on the following day it would be her main duty to aid Alwyn in his attempt to find the cause of his concerns.

Owain had spent the day, as usual, working with the prince's warriors, improving their weapon skill. He had discovered that Prince Tai's warriors now only carried spears because the Romans had recently forbidden the carrying of swords. Strictly speaking, this part of the territory of the Dubonnii was not yet part of the Empire, but recent activity further east had caused frequent incursions by heavily armed Roman detachments, and warriors carrying swords had been harshly dealt with. This had caused great resentment amongst Prince Tai's warriors, but at the prince's insistence, the men kept to spears which could be legitimately described as hunting weapons, and they kept their swords hidden in a secret cache. To Tai's relief, Owain had agreed that this was a sensible precaution, and Owain had spent the day showing the men how to best use the heavy boar spears as effective weapons.

Over their meal that night, the young Druids told Owain of the day's events and Lorchar warned Owain to treat his son sensitively as he was unsure what to feel about what the day had revealed to him. Indeed Owain felt no more sure about what to make of what had happened than did his son, and rather avoided speaking much to the young man. However, before they retired to bed, Owain drew his son aside for a quiet word. his words were terse, but the emotion behind them was clear.

'Son, remember what I said to you before. Whatever you decide to to do with what you have learned today is fine by me. I trust your judgement completely and you have my love and support, no matter what!'

Garth merely gripped his father's wrist, and gave it a squeeze of appreciation, which would have caused yelps of pain to any other man, but which only filled Owain with pride and fatherly love.

Chapter 12

Meanwhile, some way to the north and east, Marcus and Bran rode into a garrison camp of Batavian Auxiliary Cavalry. Bran had told Marcus the story of what had happened in the far west and had outlined Maelgwyn's plan to allow Marcus to gain control of Alwyn and the others. Marcus was still puzzled though.

'I am not saying I believe everything you have told me about what these young Druids can do, but if you are correct, will not this Alwyn already know of our plans?'

Bran pretended more confidence in his master's plans than he really felt. 'As I have said Marcus, this really is the optimum moment to strike. Lord Maelgwyn has discovered that the boy Alwyn and the others are now being tutored by Eirlys, the White Druid of Ynys Avalon. The work she will be doing with them will be filling much of their minds. He knows that the attack of your Legions on Mona will begin, perhaps as soon as tomorrow. When that happens, the spiritual and mental interference of those events will prevent even Alwyn from concentrating on our plans, and Maelgwyn himself is devoting all his time and energy into blocking our thoughts from Alwyn. This combination of factors gives us an unique opportunity to seize Owain from them, and use him as a lure to gain control of Alwyn and the others.' Marcus shrugged.

'Very well. I hope that your master is correct in this. I am about to introduce you to Zaba, a decurion of the Batavian Cavalry. I do not know what he will make of a request for him and his troop to accompany us to effect the capture of a veteran ex gladiator. Sixty men to capture one, and to subsequently use his men to fight off the possible attack of a bunch of apprentice Druids, including three women, two of them little more than girls. However, if I know Batavian cavalrymen the thought of those three women will be enough to bring them along with us. At the end of the day, whatever the virtues and talents of the others, it is Alwyn who is valuable to me, and his removal will be valuable to your master I gather. It may be that the boy Garth will have value as a gladiator, and the others will certainly have a price as slaves. However, if they are foolish enough to attempt the rescue of Owain, it is certain that not all of them will survive. Batavians are savage fighters!'

With that, a huge bearded man in the uniform of the Auxiliaries entered. The negotiations were protracted, and involved the drinking of more wine than Bran thought wise before a journey. However the next morning, bright and early, Bran and Marcus with sixty hulking Cavalrymen in tow clattered out of the garrison and headed towards Avalon.

After a restless and and troubled night, Alwyn was up and about early. He sought out Eirlys and Lorchar and told them of what had passed through his mind during the night.

'I told you yesterday that something perturbed me and I could not yet tell what it was. Now I know, and it is a grave concern to us all. I have seen in my mind the massed ranks of the Roman legions ranged upon the shores of the straits across from Mona, and they are boarding huge rafts to cross those straits as we speak. I have seen Myrthin and the great Druids of the island ranged across Mona's shore hurling curses, and calling on the gods to bring down ruin to the Legions. Behind them are our warriors of Mona, prepared to fight to the death to preserve what Myrthin and that island stands for. I have seen that the Roman soldiers are shaking with fear of the magic that the Druids might wreak on them, but I can also see that they are even more frightened of the wrath of their centurions, so they will fight, and Owain has taught us that in a massed battle with the Legions, there can be but one winner. So the truth is, I fear for our dear friend and teacher Myrthin, and I fear for the death of our culture, and our people forgetting the Truth in their acceptance of the peace and comfort that Romans promise along with their stone towns, their love of money and their easy Gods.'

The faces of Eirlys and Lorchar were white with shock and Lorchar's eyes brimmed with tears. It was the older Druid that spoke first. 'Alwyn, your news is not welcome, but we all, Myrthin more than all of us, knew this day was coming. That is why he sent you and the others on this venture. From events since you arrived I see just how wise he was in this. Our task today in the steam lodge is to focus all our our powers in giving what assistance we can to Mona even at this distance. You have powers way beyond anything available to the Druids on Mona. Cerna and Branwen have huge gifts, and all of us, collectively can render some assistance if we work together'

Lorchar spoke, her voice strong, though the powerful emotions running through her were obvious from the strain on her face.

'Eirlys is right. We cannot delay and we must render what assistance we can. Even if . . . . the worst comes to the worst, our mission must continue. Myrthin's sacrifice must not be in vain. Right now, to be practical we must tell the others. Two of them, in particular will be deeply affected. Branwen, does not know the truth of her birth but has for many years regarded and loved Myrthin as a father. She will be devastated at this news, but if I know her, she will turn her grief into a focussed fury that she will unleash upon the Romans. Owain, however will be harder to help. Myrthin was his oldest friend, the man who helped free him from slavery, and the man who gave him a home and a new purpose in life. He cannot help us in our Druids' work, and I know he will think he should be there today, slaying Romans, and standing at his old friend's right hand. Somehow we must convince him that he did the right thing in leading us on this mission, and that after this is over, he can best gain his revenge through helping us continue with it'

Without another word they woke the others and Alwyn told his story. Lorchar spoke urgently and with great emotion to Branwen, who emerged with a kind of blazing anger flashing from her eyes, to the great fear of the servants of the house. Eirlys and Garth spoke to Owain but he was unconsolable, eventually breaking free from the others, grabbing his cloak and his great staff and marching off into the nearby woods on his own. The others knew they had no time to waste, climbing the Tor and entering again the steam lodge.

Eirlys put new and different herbs to infuse the steam and then she and Lorchar set up a rhythmic chant that soon had most of them in a state of trance. Alwyn, however remained fully conscious as he made his mind focus on events on Mona as they occurred. Soon the others could see what Alwyn could see and even in their trance like state, each did what he or she could to render aid to the beleaguered inhabitants of Mona. Alwyn sought out Roman leaders and entered their minds, increasing their sense of panic, making them give confusing and defeatist orders. Cerna, as always picked up on emotions, and where she saw fear, she ensured that it fed and increased, allowing Legionaries to hear the screamed curses of Lorchar and Eirlys in their heads. Branwen conjured up terrifying images of wolves and bears, wild boars and screaming eagles, tearing down onto the beaches from the heights above. Branwen also caused an image of her in her guise as the Queen of Flowers to appear amongst the baggage men and their horses on the mainland, causing panic and stampedes. Garth and Pered used the power of Alwyn and Cerna to terrify the soldiers as they waded ashore on the island's beaches causing them to see frightening images of warriors with the heads of bears or hawks attacking them. The team of Druids in the steam lodge kept up this psychological attack for hours, until one by one, exhaustion, heat and hunger caused them to fall into unconsciousness. Alwyn was the last to keep going, but in the end, even he could see that force of numbers was too great and the Druids and warriors of Mona had to fall back before the inexorable might of Rome. With tears coursing down his face, he too fell into a deep and dark sleep.

Meanwhile, a few miles away, Owain was stamping and cursing his way along a forest path, smashing at bushes with his great staff, bemoaning to himself his inability to help his best friend and the peaceful island he had called home for so long. This unusual, futile raging was the thing that allowed four of the Batavian cavalrymen to get so close to Owain without him knowing. However, a snapped twig broke the spell, and Owain realised he was in danger. He gave no outward sign of this, apart form a tighter grip on the staff, and a steady control of his breathing. As the first of his would be assailants grew near, Owain whirled round to face a bearded soldier with a drawn dagger. The Batavian sprang forward but the steel headed staff flashed in the air and crashed into the cavalryman's knee with the sickening sound of breaking bone. Owain ignored this attacker now, as he rolled on the ground screaming, and faced the other three as they rushed at him together. The heavy staff whirled again, and this time broke the sword hand of one of the attackers, and then was thrust between the legs of another sending him to the forest floor. The fourth attacker closed with Owain and immediately felt the warm pain of a dagger's blade between his ribs before his life ebbed away. Owain now had the long cavalry sword in his hand as he swept it down on the tripped soldier, killing him instantly. He was about to despatch the Batavian with the smashed hand, when the word 'Enough!' was bellowed in a guttural foreign accent, and Owain turned to see a dozen armed men surrounding him, including two archers with bows taut, and arrows nocked.

The word had been uttered by a tall, broad shouldered warrior with long black hair tied back, and a full, but neat neatly trimmed black beard. Like the others, he wore a leather breastplate and leg protectors but no helmet.

The tall warrior spoke again to introduce himself. 'My name is Zaba. I am decurion of Batavian Auxiliaries and I ask you to hand over that sword'

Owain wiped the sweat from his brow and nodded an acknowledgement to Zaba, but he hung on to the sword. 'If it is your intention to kill me I would just as soon die with a sword in my hand, even if it is not one of mine.' Owain then surprised everyone by switching to fluent Latin with a distinct accent of the home city. 'I expect you are not entirely comfortable in the common British tongue and I regret I do not speak your language at all, but if you wish, I am perfectly comfortable in Latin.'

Zaba allowed himself a brief smile at the gesture. 'I thank you Owain the Gladiator, I have indeed become accustomed to Latin, and am not fluent at your language. As to the sword, whilst I appreciate the sentiment, which is one that my men and I would be completely in accord with, you should know that if we wanted you dead, you would already have your life's blood ebbing away on this ground. So with my word as to your safety, at least for today, and my assurance, that if in days to come, you are to die, it will be at my hand, and you will have a sword in yours. So sir, the sword if you please.'

Saying these words, he stepped forward boldly with his open right hand extended. Owain tossed the long cavalry sword in the air, caught it by the tip expertly and proffered the hilt to Zaba with a slight bow. The decurion bowed in return, took the sword and expertly ran it through the heart of the cavalryman with the smashed knee who had still been writhing on the ground, groaning.

'He could not have accompanied us on our return, indeed I do not believe he could have ridden with us again, better he is dead. So, Owain the Gladiator. I was warned of your prowess as a fighter, but in my arrogance I thought I knew better. How could an old man, if you will pardon the slight, of sixty summers, be the equal of four crack Batavian warriors? I was wrong. That mistake has cost me three comrades, and one who will be no good for fighting for weeks. A costly mistake indeed, but I learn quickly. You have my total respect as a worthy foe, but there is now a debt of blood between us and one day it will be repaid, believe me.'

Owain nodded. 'I do believe you sir, and I will be ready for that moment. However the fight was not mine in the first instance. Your men attacked me without provocation, I would know why, if I may'

'Indeed you shall, Owain the Gladiator, you are at least owed that courtesy' These words were spoken by one of two newcomers to the forest glade. The man who had spoken was of middle height and dressed as a Roman Legionary Officer of Tribune rank, though he did not carry himself like a soldier. The words had been spoken in perfect common British, with what Owain detected as a slight accent of the south coast, he had lived amongst the Atrebates. His companion was known to Owain, a tall saturnine young man with long, perfectly straight black hair and the coldest of pale grey eyes. Owain moved suddenly towards the pair but was instantly grabbed by strong arms, he did not resist, but spat out his hate anyway.

'Bran, you! I might have guessed that Maelgwyn would be involved in this somehow. And I suppose that the Roman who speaks such excellent British is the spy known as Marcus?'

Marcus laughed mirthlessly, 'You are well informed Owain. But on this occasion not as well informed as we are. We know all about your little party of apprentice Druids, some of whom, it seems are genuinely talented. Maelgwyn, through Bran here worked out that the only way we could make a move against you without this young seer, Alwyn knowing all about as soon as we did, was to move when his whole mind would be taken up with events on Mona. Maelgwyn intelligently guessed that you would be apart from the others on this matter, though possibly with your son. No? Well it matters not. Now we have you, and soon the others will come looking for you. We believe they value your life, and so to protect you they may well come quietly without too many magic tricks!'

Owain growled his reply. 'Well you were at least partly correct, but when those young Druids do come looking you may well regret that they have, You have no idea of the power they wield, Roman. As to affection for me, well that may be true, but they know how important their duty is too, and believe me, the Truth is greater than the affection of youth for an old warrior well able to take care of himself.'

'You disappoint me Owain, I was told by Bran here that you were a god hater like me, a rationalist, who despises all this superstition and magic nonsense. As to us regretting it when they manage to find us, I think not. With all due respect to Bran's friends, these warriors are not hotheaded simpletons. They are the finest warriors in the empire, tempered by Roman discipline. Furthermore there are sixty of them, well fifty seven now, but in any case far too many for a little band of mystics who have barely finished playing with toys, three of whom, in any case, are women. Can you imagine any woman alive who could stand up to these monsters?'

He laughed as he gestured to the Batavians. Owain replied in Latin so the cavalrymen could understand. 'You have no idea what you are up against. You are right. I was a sceptic, though I have lived amongst Druids most of my life, but the things I have seen in recent weeks have shaken me to the core.'

He turned to the Batavians and spoke to them directly, 'When they come you will not see them at first and when you do, you will wish you had not. They will turn your spines to jelly and your bowels to water. Those of you who are not horribly killed will curse your ill fortune, as you will never sleep easy again, your minds destroyed by visions you will never undo. Your families in far off lands are not safe, they too will wake and witness your death and destruction and they will curse you for the misfortune you have brought upon them'

'Enough!' Zaba's powerful voice rang out again 'You have learned to curse like a witch, but my men are not so easily frightened'

Owain looked round at the uneasy faces of the Cavalrymen, some of them trying to hide their fear in laughs and others in loud threats whilst yet others made the sign against the evil eye and he knew that Zaba was wrong and probably knew it. All of these men had been brought up in the great Rhineland forests and were afraid of the the spirits of the forest and the ancient magic, for all their professed worship of Mithras. Nevertheless, he knew better than to risk Zaba's wrath further, the seed of fear was now planted, and as he was led to a horse with his hands tied, Owain hoped and prayed that his young friends would follow soon but do it circumspectly.

It was those eyes again! Blue and intense they burned into Alwyn's mind with a cold, sharp pain like frost. At first the groggy Alwyn thought he was still in some bad dream but as he came to, he knew it was Maelgwyn, up to his old tricks, thinking he could take advantage of Alwyn's weakened state and distress about events on Mona. However, since the first time that he had been aware of Maelgwyn, Alwyn had learned a few tricks. Was that time really only a few short weeks before? So much had happened since. Alwyn carefully prepared a part of his mind that Maelgwyn could not see, and gathered up all his remaining energy, adding to it his fury at Maelgwyn and the Romans. Touching the Torc of Aneurin at his throat he physically shouted a loud 'No!' as his mind sent that message with a massive charge of energy back to hit Maelgwyn like a great blow. Alwyn actually heard the scream of pain and shock from the renegade Druid and then nothing. Alwyn knew that Maelgwyn had been knocked unconscious by the mental shock, but he was not killed. He would recover but Alwyn doubted that he would ever again attempt to probe the young Druid's mind.

The great shout woke the others. They were still lying in the steam lodge though the fire had long since gone out, and they all pulled the blankets around themselves in the cool night air. All of them were hungry, thirsty and a little disheartened that they had not been able to do more to help Myrthin and the others on Mona. Naturally enough, knowing of Alwyn's prescience, they feared the worst from the great shout of 'No' from him. He reassured them that he was unaware of any harm to their old friend and mentor. Just then Alwyn was struck with a great sense of unease. He silenced the others and focussed his mind sharply. After a few minutes he gave a great moan. Lorchar spoke first, with a catch in her voice. 'Is it Myrthin? Have you just learned something?'

Alwyn had tears in his eyes as he replied. 'No, no, not Myrthin, now it is Owain in danger. Whilst we lay here exhausted and sleeping, he has been captured by a large group of Roman cavalry. I see Maelgwyn's henchman, Bran and a man in a Roman officer's dress, Bran is calling him Marcus. It is the spy we heard of in King Maelor's land. I see it now. We have been the victims of one of Maelgwyn's clever plots. He knew that we would be absorbed in trying to help Mona at this time and gambled that we, or rather I, would miss a lesser plot to capture Owain, who would lack our rather special protection.'

Garth was on his feet by now, his blanket kilted round his waist and his muscular frame tense with fury. 'But why do they want Father ? What use is he to them? My God it must have cost them dear to capture him alive'

Alwyn replied in a flat, matter of fact voice. 'It did, three dead and one badly injured. It has not endeared him to his captors. But he is safe for now because the real target is us, especially me. We know how Maelgwyn hates and fears us, well, he has persuaded this Marcus that there is advantage and profit in it for him if he can capture us. He hopes to do so with Owain as hostage'

Branwen gave a harsh, humourless laugh at this. 'Do they not know what we can do? We will destroy them and in a most horrible way. Just point us in the right direction Alwyn and they will discover what it is to incur the wrath of Druids!'

Alwyn spoke with a calm he did not feel inside. 'We must not rush headlong into this. We must plan and move with care. There are some sixty of these men, wild and fierce looking they are, men from Germania, I judge, but professionals, Roman trained. They will have detailed men to ride alongside Owain, to kill him if they must. But they think that with him, they have all they need to secure us, so they will not harm him rashly. In one thing you are right Branwen, they have no conception of what we can do, indeed we do not really know our own limits yet. They are a few hours ahead of us but now they are halting for the night. We must not let them get Owain inside a Roman Garrison. Our best bet is the forest and that is your domain Branwen. I sense these foreign soldiers are of the forest themselves, so they will have a healthy fear of it we can exploit. Lady Eirlys, we need to eat to restore our energy and we need to gather some supplies and horses. We will not take local soldiers, if things go wrong it would bring retribution on all the Dubonnii. I feel a plan of action is forming in my mind, one that will require all the special skills that each of us can bring, but I need to talk it over with all of you to see if you feel you can do what I ask of you.'

Garth, white with fury at the seizure of his father was champing at the bit to be after the Romans immediately, but Eirlys and Lorchar sat with him and calmed him, reassuring him that Alwyn was right, a carefully thought out plan following a meal and thorough preparations was the best way forward.

During their hurried meal Alwyn sat with the two older Druids, in urgent discussion whilst the others concocted wild and unfeasible plans, and outlined the terrible fate that would befall any Roman who harmed Owain. Cerna sat apart however, eating in a desultory manner but with her mind clearly elsewhere. When the meal was over and they all gathered together around the large table in the Prince's hall, it was Cerna who spoke first.

'As you all know I am sensitive to the feelings and emotions of others, and whilst we ate, I sent my mind out to those who hold Owain. In the main they are afraid. Alwyn is right, these horse soldiers, Batavians they call themselves, are people of the forest and they are very superstitious. It seems that Owain has spoken and placed a few fears in their heads. They are talking amongst themselves. They have heard much about Druids and they fear what they have heard. Bran, Maelgwyn's man is there. He is saying little but he too is afraid, he has heard what happened to Maelgwyn's soldiers. He is terrified of the fact that Maelgwyn has not tried to contact him mentally, in many hours. He was relying on a warning from his master if we came near. Only two people in the group have no fear. One is Owain, who knows we will come, and that we will prevail. I must tell you that he he has prepared himself for death, if need be, as long as we do not fall into the hands of the Romans. The other one who is not afraid is Marcus, the spy. He seems to be a matter of fact, unsuperstious sort, who fears no magic or spirits because he has no experience of them. I have taken it upon myself to plant a few fears in his mind, where they will fester through the night. Few of them will sleep well tonight.'

Alwyn permitted himself a smile at this before speaking himself. 'Well done Cerna, that is useful intelligence. Owain's captors are several hours ahead of us and though we can set off soon, and regain a few hours on them, we cannot permit them to retain this start they have on us. We must catch them in the forest to be successful. Now it seems to me that two of our number can bridge the gap between us in no time at all. Both Branwen and Pered have the power to transform themselves into birds that can fly that distance in a short time. Branwen you can take on the spirit of the of the white owl and can guide Pered as the goshawk, until it is light, when he can use the speed and forest flying skill of the hawk to locate our enemies. When they are found, he can come back and let us know, whilst Branwen can use her invisibility and her power in the forest to, shall we say, hinder these Batavians, as well as using these powers to increase their fears to the point where they will be in a state of terror already when we arrive. Obviously

Cerna and I will be filling their minds with the most nameless terrors the whole while. What do you two say?'

Pered and and Branwen looked at each other questioningly and it was Pered who spoke first, more hesitant than Alwyn had ever seen him.

'Look, for the last two days I have been dying to try out this transformation, I have always felt an affinity for the great forest hawk. But in truth, I had hoped for a practice before taking on the transformation in earnest, as it were. I mean, I have never transformed before, what it will it be like to fly when I have never done it? Who will show me how to transform back? I know Branwen has some experience of transformation but she has never become a bird. You all know that I am afraid of no-one and nothing, and I would lay down my life for Owain, or any of you in a second, but I do confess I am afraid of taking on this vital task and not being able to properly execute it.'

Lorchar quickly interjected. 'Pered my boy, you have nothing to fear. I have never been able to transform into anything but the wolf, though I would love to fly, but I can tell you this. When you transform, you do not become an ordinary animal, you have absorbed the spirit, the very essence of the creature. You retain your own mind whilst the spirit of the creature deals with those aspects of the creature you have no experience of. When I am a wolf I can interpret a million smells my human nose could not even detect. I did not have to learn that skill. As a wolf I can run all day at a speed my human self could not match for a few hundred yards. As a wildcat Branwen can see in the dark, a skill she loses instantly when she transforms back to human. When the two of you, if you agree, transform into birds you will already know how to fly and navigate, whilst retaining at all times your human intelligence and sense of who you are and what you are about. So, you two, what do you say? Are you up for it?'

Branwen gave her usual mad grin and just said 'When do we start?'.

Pered looked at her for a second, laughed and said 'No time like the present! Lorchar, Eirlys, show us how to do it!'

Alwyn raised a hand, though his face was wreathed in smiles. 'One moment, you mad, impetuous pair. This is what you must do. You both fly off and find them. Branwen, though you are the youngest of us, you have immense powers, and I know I can trust you to use them wisely. The Batavians, or whatever they are called must be delayed. They must be thoroughly scared, but they must not be so desperate they attempt to kill Owain, though I know you have many ways to protect him. Pered, after a short rest you must transform back to the hawk, to lead us to to our enemies, where we will bring to bear our full range of powers. Is that understood?'

The tall, proud boy and the slight, energetic girl nodded their agreement and went outside with Lorchar, Eirlys and Cerna. Alwyn rose to follow when he was detained by the massive hand of Garth.

'Garth, you mean only to talk to me, I know, but you are crushing my arm in your anxiety. What troubles you my friend?'

Garth reddened and released Alwyn's arm, but his anxiety was still etched in his handsome face. 'Alwyn, it is my father that is in the hands of these soldiers and we did not part on the best of terms. I love him dearly but I feel powerless in this situation. It is you and Cerna, Branwen and Pered taking the initiative and Lorcha too. I have inherited so little of my mother's powers I feel helpless in this situation. What can I do?'

Alwyn looked at him kindly.'At this distance, it is true, our powers are of more value, but soon we must come face to face with these formidable warriors. We now lack your father's knowledge and skills, we will rely on you to tell us how to proceed in the deadly face to face meeting. Besides, do not underestimate the power you have inherited from your mother. You cannot fully transform into the bear as yet, but you can take on all the powers of the bear. When you do, as inevitably you will have to, the effect on these forest dwellers from a land where the bear is still common will be decisive, believe me!'

Garth smiled sadly. 'What you say is true, I am sure, but it is very hard now, with my father taken, to watch whilst others plan the path to free him, but I will do as Eirlys has advised and store this frustration up to be released at a time when I can put that anger and frustrated energy to real use'

Alwyn clapped a hand on the young warrior's huge shoulder and led him out to join the others. All of them gathered in a small circle around Branwen and Pered. These two were white faced and anxious. Even Branwen, with her love of excitement was in awe at the strangeness and enormity of what she was about to undertake. Even Pered's normally unshakeable self confidence was deserting him at the thought of becoming a bird, and flying many miles over strange terrain to meet a powerful and dangerous enemy. Alwyn went straight to Branwen and gripped both arms of the young girl. Emotion made his normally calm voice shake as he quietly spoke to her.

'Branwen, you are the bravest of us all, but in this enterprise you must be careful and look after yourself and Pered, he is inclined to be hotheaded. We must do all we can to save Owain but I . . . I would be very sad if, if anything should happen to you.'

He flushed and his normally calm face shook with emotion that he hid by turning away. Branwen's heart turning cartwheels at the thought that this brilliant, but self possessed young Druid cared what happened to her, and she could have faced a whole legion of Batavians at that moment. Lorchar and Eirlys now stepped forward and muttered words of advice and confidence in Branwen and Pered's abilities, though both knew they were about to witness something that no Druid had seen in Britain in living memory. They were sustained though, by that depth of oral knowledge that was the secret of the Druids' success for so many centuries. Both of them knew that this had been done before and done successfully and they passed this knowledge and encouragement to the two frightened young people in front of them. They taught Branwen and and Pered to focus on the spirit of the white owl and the forest hawk as they saw it and taught them the words to say to call on that spirit. As before, the air around them began to shake and grow misty. As it cleared the two birds stood on the clothes of the two Druids who had previously occupied that space and they flapped their wings and called after the manner of their kind. Branwen and Pered were delighted to realise that they could understand each other's thoughts and those of the other Druids, with Alwyn's coming in most strongly. They also realised that they knew perfectly well how to fly and to navigate, and they were filled with a new confidence.

They flapped their wings more strongly and rose into the air with ease. In the still dark sky, Branwen with her well developed night vision took the lead, and Pered followed close behind, keeping the white owl well in sight. They were well aware of the good wishes of the others crowding in on them until they put some distance between them and the other Druids, until only Alwyn's clear thoughts reminding them of the task in hand came through, though they were also aware of the feeling of well being that came from Cerna's sensitive mind.

The two spirit birds flew on. In the east they could perceive the gradual lightening of the sky which spurred them on. They wanted to reach the Batavian's camp before the soldiers rose. In due course, just as the sun imparted a faint pink to the east, the owl that was Branwen dropped down to a treetop, followed by the hawk that was Pered. Branwen's thoughts let Pered know that she could sense Owain's presence in the thick forest down below. Sure enough, Pered's keen eyes, even in the faint light of dawn, could make out smouldering fires and the dull shape of tents. The two spirit birds flew a little way off, and created that disturbance of the air that indicated a return to their real shapes. The morning was still cold, but their exertions meant they did not feel the cold despite their lack of clothes. Branwen was full of urgency and purpose.

'I can go back down to the camp protected by my invisibility. I need to establish that Owain is still alright, and if I can, to reassure him that he is found, and help will soon be at hand. I also intend to create a little mischief down there and put a few fresh fears into the hearts and minds of those soldiers, if I can. What I suggest is that you return to the shape of the hawk and fly down to watch events. Once you have seen that Owain is alive and well, and you have picked up any intelligence you think may be useful, it would be best if you returned to the others to guide them here. I do not think that in this forest I can come to any harm and indeed I may be able to use the creatures and plants of the forest to sew even more fear and discord amongst our enemies.'

It hurt Pered's considerable pride to have the brash young Branwen guide his actions in this way, but he recognised that here in the forest,

Branwen was Queen, and she had the powers and skills not only to survive, but to do real damage to their enemies. He knew she was right and besides the cold morning, and his own self consciousness reminded him of his nakedness, and he did not feel entirely comfortable. However he did think that his own powers could make a contribution beyond that of being a mere messenger. Quickly, he outlined his suggestion.

'A good plan, Branwen, which we should set in motion without delay. I have one small suggestion though. Once you have begun causing a little confusion, I believe I can make an useful contribution to it. What if I can use one of my voices of power to increase their fear by doing it whilst still in the body of the Hawk.'

Branwen frowned. 'But can you do that ?, Surely you need the voice of a man for that, and the hawk does not have it!'

Pered smiled triumphantly, 'True, Branwen, but one of my new found skills is to produce that voice inside men's minds and make them believe it is spoken aloud. I can make them believe that the voice is coming from the beak of the great hawk they see in the branches nearby, whose beak is opening and closing as if speaking!'

Branwen did a little silent dance of glee as she thought of the horror this phenomenon would create. 'Brilliant Pered! but listen' Her voice grew serious again. 'We must remember our main task here, to free Owain, only when that is done will it be safe to send these Batavians screaming for their mothers off into the forest. You must get the message back to the others for we need their help. As soon as you see anyone reach for a bow or a sling you must fly off at once!'

Pered seemed hurt that Branwen should think him capable of forgetting his duty.

'I think that I know what my first duty is Branwen' Seeing her face fall, Pered relented. 'But I thank you for thinking of my safety and for reminding me that Owain's safety must come first. Come then, let's be about it.'

Within seconds Branwen disappeared from sight entirely in a shiver of greenish hues whilst Pered summoned up the spirit of the hawk again and flew down to the camp with the speed through the branches only a goshawk could produce. He sat on a branch at the edge of the encampment to await developments. Branwen had made her own invisible way down into the edge of the camp. She made not a sound as she crept past the bleary eyed sentry into the centre of the encampment. Only the horses seemed aware of her presence, whinnying slightly until Branwen sent out calming thoughts. The soldier on horse picket duty looked around keenly for a few moments, but then dismissed the disturbance as some forest creature passing by. A few tired looking soldiers were rising now to revive the fires and make a little porridge for the men. The invisible young Druid moved from tent to tent peering in through the flaps. In due course she found the one she was looking for. Owain was lying there, his eyes wide open, his hands tied together over his blanket. There were two guards in the tent. One beginning to bestir himself, the other fast asleep.

Branwen made a brief noise outside the tent and the guard who was awake rushed outside, kicking the other awake as he went. When both were outside, searching for the disturbance, Branwen went in and placed her hand on Owain's mouth. She made her face faintly visible to him, and silently made him understand that they had found him, and help was on its way. Owain smiled gently at his friend and urged her to leave the tent. Becoming invisible again, Branwen left the tent as the two guards re-entered, deliberately tripping one of them up as she went.

Hiding behind the tents, Branwen briefly made herself visible as she signalled to Pered that Owain was alive and well. The Hawk in the branches turned its fierce orange eyes onto Branwen and flapped its wings to show it understood. Becoming invisible again, Branwen, took a deep breath and smiled a tense smile. Now was the time to create a little havoc, and spread some fear into the hearts of these tough soldiers. She silently made her way over to the horse picket area of the camp. Once again her presence slightly spooked the horses, and the guard moved to check on them. Branwen picked up a heavy stone and struck the soldier on the back of the head. He slumped to the ground, unconscious. Branwen took his sharp dagger and moved among the horses, freeing them from their tethers. She shouted and clapped her hands, and the horses took off, running into the dense forest.

Now cavalrymen were running in from all directions, pulling on tunics and freeing swords from scabbards, shouting as they ran.

The young Druid noted three people in particular, because they were so different. A tall, broad soldier with a beard and long dark hair, sword in hand, whose shouted commands were instantly obeyed, was accompanied by a stocky man with short, Roman style hair and a tunic like Owain's, his face black with fury. The third man was slim, rangy with long, glossy black hair and pale grey eyes, dressed in the British fashion. This man must be Bran, Maelgwyn's crony, whilst the Roman must be the spy known as Marcus and the big man was obviously the Batavian commander. They gathered by the picket, taking in the stunned guard and the cut tethers. Soldiers were sent out in groups to recover the horses. Branwen wasted no further time, she ran to Owain's tent, where one guard had been left outside to ensure that the gladiator did not escape. Branwen picked up a dropped dagger and moved invisibly closer to the guard. Creeping up behind him, she placed one hand over his mouth whilst cutting his throat with the sharp dagger. She slipped into the tent and made herself visible again. Urgently, she spoke to her friend.

'Look Owain, it will be a few hours before the others get here, so I cannot release you yet, You would not be able to escape these soldiers, but I have created enough disruption to delay them leaving with you quite yet. You need to know that you are our first priority, and I will personally ensure no harm comes to you. I will leave you this knife to hide and use if the need arises.'

Owain smiled fondly at this tiny figure that was going to protect him. 'Thank you Branwen, but I need you all to know that I regard myself expendable in way that you are not. I have lived my life to the full, and should have died a hundred times already. I have no special virtues or powers, and I cannot save our culture, so do not risk yourself for me'

Branwen smiled back as she disappeared again, 'You do have one special virtue Owain the Gladiator, you are our friend!'

Owain hid the knife in his boot as he heard the rustle of the guard's body being dragged into the undergrowth by Branwen.

Pered had now decided to add to the confusion in the camp with his own special talent. He concentrated hard and soon soldiers who were running around stopped dead and looked around as they heard a loud sibilant whisper in their own language issuing terrible threats and curses.

'Call yourself Batavian warriors, you are a disgrace. Look at you running around a forest, capturing an old man, so you can kill priests and children at the behest of an accursed Roman! Well now you have gone too far, you are disturbing the spirits of this ancient forest, and you know what that means! The Forest itself will turn on you, the very roots of the trees will grow through your bodies after the animals and birds have chewed on your bones and the worms crawled through your empty eye sockets. You will never see your heaven, because the forest spirits will bar your entrance. Your spirits will be condemned to wander these isles forever, knowing no rest. But the spirits of the forest will not be content with this, no, they will seek out your families and torment them with images of your terrible death and the horrors you will undergo for eternity, and it will send them all mad with grief and terror. Will you undergo all this for the sake of the Romans who even now destroy your own land? If you do not believe me, if you seek a sign that I speak only truth. Look up into the branches now, see the great hawk there, see his beak, he is speaking. The spirit of the Forest Hawk who sees all, is the one speaking to you. Witness this and tremble!'

Soldiers all round the camp now were frozen in terror, most looking up at the Goshawk in the trees flapping his wings and fixing individuals with those terrible fierce amber eyes. Not all were silent though, some were muttering payers and making signs against the evil eye whilst yet others whispered to their fellows that this was not an honourable mission and they would not risk the anger of the Forest Gods. Even the three leaders were not immune from fear of the whispering horror that they heard in their heads, but it was Marcus who broke the spell.

'Enough!' he bellowed 'These are nothing but Druid tricks, Bran here will tell you how they are done. These Druid children know they cannot face us, so they are trying to scare us with magic tricks, and it seems they are succeeding. Call yourself mighty warriors, yet you jump at shadows? You there!' he shouted at a young soldier who carried a bow and arrow, 'Take that bow and put an arrow through that hawk, it is no spirit just a forest hawk, the rest is sorcery!'

The young man reluctantly raised the bow and as he did so a heavy log chopped for the fire flew through the air, and smashed into his face, knocking him flat. The hawk took off and disappeared through the dense forest. The soldiers muttered again and this time it was Zaba, their leader who shouted at them.

'More trickery! Fools! Are you going to stand here all day shaking in your boots, whilst your horses run further off into the forest. Organise yourselves into fours and find those horses. I warn you now, I will chase any deserters until I die, and when I catch them they will wish they were facing the fate described by the Druids' curse. Go now, jump to it!'

The spell, having to some extent been broken, groups of soldiers dutifully ran off to search for their horses. Zaba wiped sweat from his brow and spoke through clenched teeth as he addressed Bran. 'Well Briton, explain it, you work for a Druid of some power I am told, how was the trick done?'

Bran smiled nervously, 'You must understand that there are genuine powers here, though I know friend Marcus here is dismissive. But I think I can explain some of it. What language did you hear the message in?'

The decurion grunted, 'In my own tongue of course, my own dialect come to think of it.' 'And you Marcus?' The Roman thought for a moment, 'Well Latin, but now I recall it was Latin with the same mix of Gaulish and Atrebate accent that I use myself'

'Exactly, and I heard it in the Decanglii version of the British tongue that is native to me. Can you not see that none of us really heard that message at all, it was put into our minds by power of thought? Alwyn certainly has that power and he can do it at a distance too. I cannot explain the hawk, or how the horses were released, but as I say, do not doubt that these young Druids have powers we can but dream of, else why would you want them alive Marcus'

Zaba spat on the ground with disgust 'Well all of that may be so, but I warn you Marcus, you had better succeed with this plan because with nothing to show for the loss of men and horses, my Tribune will have me disemboweled in front of my men, and the only thing that will sustain me as I slowly die will be that I will have already done the same to you'

By now Branwen, still invisible to all her enemies, was sitting up in the broad bough of an oak tree outside the camp, watching the cavalrymen stumble through the dense undergrowth beneath her as they searched for their missing horses. On the branch in front of her Branwen spread out a number of items, and began a low chant, that could not be heard on the forest floor below. In front of her she had a boar's tusk, a tuft of wolf hair, a length of bramble, a strip of dried out deer antler velvet and some tree rots. She picked up each item in turn, and if you could have seen her face you would have witnessed intense concentration as she chanted her incantations. In the forest below, her spells came to fruition.

A group of four Batavians crashed through the forest as they followed signs of their missing horses. They heard some answering crashes, and a group of wild boar broke out into the same small clearing as the four men. The men were not concerned. They were forest people themselves, they knew that Boar were only dangerous when cornered, though sows with young were to be avoided. This was a group of young males. Startled by the men, they would flee back into the safety of the undergrowth. This group did not behave to expectation. They looked at the men and without hesitation charged straight at them. The soldiers, shocked by this, turned and fled. Three of them sustained nasty wounds to their legs, the fourth, who fell, was gored in his vital organs and screamed as he lay dying until one of his limping fellows put him out of his agonies.

Another group were even more shocked when they came upon a pack of five wolves. To see wolves at this time of year, and in daylight at this low elevation in southern Britain was unheard of, but the men knew what to do. They shouted and waved their swords in the air. The wolves would run away. Not these wolves, they snarled, held their ground and even moved forward. The four men stood back to back, swords drawn, and still the wolves came on. They darted in and snapped at the soldiers' bare legs, jumping back as the swords were swung. All four men were soon bleeding from bites, but when one of them managed to kill a wolf, the other wolves finally slunk away into the forest.

A third group seemed to find themselves in a particularly dense area of undergrowth, and soon they were using their long swords to hack a path through it. Several times they tried to turn and retrace their steps, but the path they had so arduously cleared, seemed to have closed up behind them. The brambles, thorn bushes and gorse now seemed to be head high and all four men were bleeding profusely from a thousand scratches. Just when they almost despaired of escaping they finally broke through into a clearing where all four lay for almost an hour exhausted, frightened and bleeding.

Whilst this was happening a fourth group had actually found some of the horses and were approaching them with soft, cajoling words when a young red deer stag broke into the small clearing they were crossing. The stag snorted and pawed the ground and immediately charged straight into the soldiers. They succeeded in killing the stag but not before one of their number, pierced by the sharp antlers of the stag had expired in front of his shocked friends.

Yet another group of four was in an area of the forest that was fairly open beech wood. They could hear some horses not too far away, and so were moving quickly towards the sound. One of their number, in his haste, tripped over a tree root and fell heavily. His friends cursed him, and went towards him to drag him to his feet. As they approached, there was a terrible sound that seemed to emanate from the ground beneath their feet. To their stunned amazement they saw the ground around their fallen friend yawn open and swallow him whole. They rushed up and dug frantically with their swords and hands, but strangely the ground, which had opened so suddenly would not now yield up the missing soldier. They began to hear again that same terrible underground sound, and they leapt to their feet and fled.

Eventually, two or more hours after they had all left the camp the soldiers that had survived the ordeal returned. Only twenty four horses had so far been found, but far more damaging to morale, was the return of shocked and bleeding fellows with tales of animals and even the forest itself behaving in an uncharacteristic way, malevolent to these forest born soldiers, whose deepest superstitions and fears were now aroused, as they heard the sum of these tales. They remembered the frightening stories told to them by grandmothers long ago, and they shivered at the thought of another night in this benighted forest and all its its strange terrors. Zaba was almost beside himself with rage.

'How in the name of all the Gods am I explain this disaster to my Tribune, Marcus? I have lost more than half my horses and several men in ways I cannot account for. Many more of my men are injured and all are now in a state of terror that borders on hysteria. One more unexplained occurrence will send them over the edge, and these Druids have not even made contact yet. You got me in to this mess Marcus, you had better have a plan to get us out of it or I swear you will not walk out of this forest a whole man!'

Marcus looked at the raging soldier with ill disguised contempt. 'Do not presume to threaten me decurion. I chose you and your Batavians because I was told they were the bravest, more fearsome soldiers in Britain. And now what do I find? A few Druid conjuring tricks, and a few sly killings, and they are all shaking in their boots and you are stamping around shouting and issuing futile threats. I am deeply unimpressed!'

Zaba's scarred face went from a strong red to white with fury at this insult. He stepped up to much shorter Roman spy and grabbing a handful of his tunic lifted him bodily off his feet, his beard just inches from Marcus' clean shaven face. To his credit, Marcus did not change his expression, and he showed no fear. Indeed, his left hand was moving round to a small sheath at the back of his belt where a short dagger was concealed. Bran watched this with increasing horror. If Marcus attempted, let alone succeeded in killing the furious decurion, neither Marcus or Bran would leave the forest alive. With considerable speed, Bran leaped forward and separated the two snarling figures of the spy and and the auxiliary officer.

'Can you two not see that in fighting amongst ourselves, we are doing the Druids' work for them? Listen to me! if we stick together, this group of

Druids, for all their powers cannot defeat us. Marcus is dismissive of the so called magical power of these young people, but I have seen Druidic mind games in action and I tell you they are very real. Even my master, who was the most gifted of his generation, is wary of the powers of these youngsters, and I cannot begin to explain what has happened today, but we still hold the whip hand as long as we have the old gladiator in our power. They will not want to see him harmed, so in the end they will do our bidding. Zaba, if I were you I would forget the horses, they will, in the main find their way back to the others here in due course. Gather all your men around us here, and bring Owain, bound and gagged to join us. When the Druids show their hand we will issue our threat to the old man and make our demands. I do not expect them to give way immediately. We may have to cause a little blood to flow from Owain first. In the end their tender hearts will ensure our victory!'

Marcus smoothed down his crumpled tunic front and grunted. 'The Briton is right Zaba, we have nothing to gain and everything to lose from fighting amongst ourselves. Give those orders to your men.'

Zaba, still breathing hard in his anger, stared at Marcus a long while, indicating their quarrel was put aside but not forgotten, With an effort, he controlled himself and reluctantly agreed with Bran. 'You do speak with some sense Briton. I will do as you suggest'

With a few shouted commands in his guttural native tongue, soldiers began to appear, carrying their weapons and tethering the remaining horses in the same clearing. Three armed soldiers were detailed to go to fetch Owain from his tent. Meanwhile however, Branwen who had been carefully watching events, had already sneaked into the tent to forewarn Owain.

'Come on, we must leave now, I will cut your bonds with that knife I gave you and we will escape before the soldiers arrive. They intend to harm you if Lorchar and Alwyn and the others do not accede to their demands. Quickly now, move yourself'

Owain grinned at Branwen, who was almost beside herself with impatience.

'No my dear, that cannot be the way. I can still fight like a much younger man, but I must confess that my running days are over, especially after being bound for so long. They would catch me up in minutes, and I cannot hide as you can. No, forewarned is forearmed, I will go along with them, and when the time comes, if need be, I will free myself and kill their leaders. With the mind wars you and your friends will doubtless wage, the rest of the soldiers will run away in abject fear. Your first task must be to warn the others of the situation so that they can plan accordingly. Above all, warn them to attempt nothing foolhardy. These are tough, experienced soldiers, and in adversity they will fight to the death. You must all find ways to make them fear you and your powers more than they fear death. Now I hear my guards approach, disappear again and then find the others. Do not fear for me!'

Branwen's eyes blazed though tears ran down her cheeks. 'If they harm one hair of your head Owain, they will wish that they had died first, I will have them envy the dead. That I promise!'

With that fearsome threat Branwen disappeared again before the guards returned to the tent. In their fear and anger at what had happened already, the guards were far rougher with Owain as they dragged him to the clearing where the rest of the soldiers had gathered. As they forced him to his knees before the three leaders. Owain addressed his remarks to Marcus, knowing this would irritate Zaba.

'Well, it would appear that you have suffered some unaccountable bad luck since last we spoke yesterday. A lot less horses about, and a few less men unless I am mistaken. Ah well! The forest is a dangerous place, is it not Marcus? And Zaba, you will pardon me for saying so, but your men seem a little, well, jumpy today, do they not? Where has all that arrogance of yesterday gone? Do not tell me they are scared of a few young priests?'

Zaba stepped forward and slapped the gladiator, hard, with the back of his hand, bringing blood to the old man's lips.

Owain merely smiled, coldly. 'Is this the famed Batavian courage then, hitting a man twice your age, when he is tied up and unable to strike back?'

Zaba ground his teeth together in fury 'I swear, old man, that before this day is over I will free you of your bonds, put a sword in your hands, and you and I will will test each other's courage and skill.' 'More brave words than deeds Zaba' replied the Gladiator.

Marcus interrupted. 'Enough love words between you two. Owain the Gladiator, you only live because you can bring us the young Druids. If they do not agree to our demands, you will die a painful death, that I promise. We may have to damage you a little first, if your friends are reluctant to parley. In the meantime we will wait here, in silence until your friends put in an appearance'

Branwen, having transformed back to the white owl, found her friends quite quickly and appraised them of the situation regarding Owain and the soldiers.

'. . . . So you see, Owain is in some danger, we must get back to protect him soon' The breathless girl, with Lorchar's cloak around her to keep her warm, finished with this demand. Alwyn, as was his way, remained silent while he thought things through. Eventually, he spoke.

'Hmm, I see what you are saying Branwen, but it seems to me that, although his situation is not a good one, it only really gets dangerous when we do get there. Until then, Marcus will protect what he sees as his only way to control us. When we do get there, I am confident that we have the skills and powers to protect him from harm, but extricating him from all those angry soldiers will be a more difficult task. Lorchar, Garth, you have more experience than I in these tactical situations, what do you think?'

It was Garth, breathing hard to control his fury at the way his father was being treated, that spoke first. 'There are still too many of them to launch an all out attack. Besides it might involve you, Cerna and Branwen too much and we need you to give my father the protection only your powers can give. We need to whittle away at the soldiers' confidence, scare them into deserting Marcus and Bran. I know what I can do in that regard, but you my friends, you grow in power day by day. I hardly know what you might be capable of. Lorchar, you are older and more experienced than any of us. What say you?'

Lorchar touched Garth's arm gently, aware of the struggle that must be happening in that mighty chest.

'I think you are right Garth. Those of you with powers to affect men's hearts and minds at a distance must use the time until we approach their camp to spread fear and despondency in any way you can. When we arrive there, we must think of something special to convince them that they are dealing with very powerful beings they should not have angered. Once we make ourselves known, they will want to communicate directly with you Alwyn, which might affect your ability to continue to damage them. At that point, Branwen and Cerna you must make it your business to protect Owain from harm. while the rest of us continue to make the soldiers lives a hell they are desperate to escape from. Alwyn, you see into men's minds better than anyone. When the time comes that only all out attack will do, give us the signal. Garth will lead the attack. Not only is he the seasoned warrior amongst us, I think his new found powers will cause even the toughest Batavian to lose control of his bowels!'

Alwyn grinned. 'A good plan Lorchar! So, Cerna you and I will spread a little fear and uncertainty in the broad breasts of these cavalrymen. Meanwhile you Branwen, along with Lorchar, Pered and Garth can be planning what shocks we can give them when we approach their camp. The rest we have to leave to the spirits we serve by following the Truth!'

At the Batavian camp, all was not well with the waiting cavalrymen. Thoughts of home sent some into sobs of sorrow and homesickness. Others vomited with unvoiced fears. Still others chatted uncontrollably of magic, of feared shamen back home and the effects of their terrible curses. Some sat and sang such sad songs of the homeland, that it made others fight with them to shut them up. At the edges, twos and threes slipped away into the dark forest. Even its dangers paled into insignificance against the horrors that forced their way into their minds and emotions. Zaba marched up and down and roared at his men, to little effect. Even Marcus seemed sad and subdued. It was Bran, with his experience of the work of Druids, who first realised what was happening. He shook off his own growing fears and sadness, jumped to his feet and yelled out.

'We are under attack, not from spears and arrows but the mental powers of powerful Druids. We must fight and keep active, or they will destroy us before they are even near!'

Zaba got all the men to their feet, made them check their weapons, practice fighting, moved them up and down, stopped them from brooding. Marcus seized the bound Owain by his tunic front.

'What is happening gladiator? Make them stop these mind games or I swear you will pay the price!'

Owain laughed in the stocky Roman's face.'You chose to play this game Marcus, now you must face the hazards. You did not really believe in the powers of these young people. A few weeks ago I confess I shared your scepticism, now I know more. I guess that now it is your turn to learn. These Druids have real power over minds, and over nature. You have bitten off more than you can chew. Your best chance is, that as Druids, they do not bear grudges. Leave me here, unharmed and you will escape with your life and your mind intact. Persist with this folly and and your men will be destroyed, and you will suffer the horrors of Hades before you too meet a terrible end. The choice is yours'

Marcus snarled in reply.'Give me one reason why I should not start chopping bits off you now, giving a warning to your friends what the result would be if they do not desist with these cowardly attacks on the minds of simple soldiers!'

Owain did not look worried. 'Marcus, Marcus, you persist in underestimating your enemy. However did you rise in your profession? I fought, undefeated, in the arenas of Rome for fifteen years. I faced more fearsome foes than you on a daily basis. It has been many years since I last feared death and pain is an old friend to me. Take out your dagger and do your worst. See what happens!'

Marcus snatched at the hilt of his dagger. To his amazement he could not pull it from its sheath. He looked back at Owain and saw instead his father's face. His father had been dead for ten years. He screamed and covered his eyes. Zaba watched this exchange with growing amazement.

'Why, in the name of the Bull did I allow myself to be dragged into this horror? At the last count I had only thirty two men left! Thirty two out of sixty, and my men have not even drawn one drop of British blood yet! We are just simple soldiers, we are not equipped to fight against magic and games of the mind. Bran you are a Briton and one who has worked with a powerful Druid, what can we do?'

Bran, wide eyed shook his head. 'I have seen much, but nothing like this. No wonder my master wanted rid of this boy and his friends, but I fear he acted too late.'

It was then that the noise began. At first it was just like the normal noise of the forest, somewhat magnified. The calls of birds and animals, the creak of the branches. But soon it began to grow, and sounds they should not hear at this time of day, or this time of year, in volumes and numbers unimaginable, began to manifest themselves. They heard the call of a wolf, then another and another. Soon there seemed to be hundreds surrounding the camp. The screams of lynx, wildcat and fox followed, and the noise of the trees was almost unbearable. There was no wind, yet the trees creaked and groaned like dying men, and the noise grew and grew. Then came the crows. In their hundreds, rooks, jackdaws, carrion cows, magpies, ravens, more and more, until their noise filled the glade. Soldiers were screaming and covering their ears. Then, silencing the sounds of nature, came the voice.

The voice spoke in the native tongue of the Batavians. Powerful and persuasive, it filled their minds as it told them the old tales of their forest homeland. The voice explained that all forests were connected, and the spirits of the forest were displeased with them. The voice told them that their families back home were vulnerable to the anger of the forest spirits, who would seek vengeance if they did not immediately vacate this place and flee.

And flee they did, another thirteen of them. Leaving less than twenty men including the three leaders. It was Zaba who broke the spell. 'Enough!' He yelled. 'We end this now, kill the gladiator!'

Zaba's second in command, the troop's optio, hauled Owain to his feet and reached for his dagger, ready to do his chief's bidding. As he did so, the man realised that the hilt of his dagger glowed the dull red of hot metal, and his hand felt the searing burn. With a scream, the optio dropped the dagger and fell, sobbing with pain, to his knees. Bran drew his sword and advanced on Owain. Then he saw that his sword was actually a viper and threw it aside with a terrified yell. Zaba saw how it was and made a fateful decision.

'Very well Owain the Gladiator, your friends have magic too powerful for us mere soldiers. So let us settle matters as men should, Face to face, with swords in our hands. Tell your friends to hold back the sorcery, and let us fight man to man. I accept that I will not leave this glade alive, but let me end it as a warrior should.'

Owain laughed.'You are very brave to fight a man twice your age Zaba. But I wonder if you know what you take on here. I am old now, it is true, but I am still fit, and fighting on foot, one on one is what I have done all my life. You are brave, but you are cavalry. How will you fare in a hand to hand battle on foot?

Zaba sneered in reply, 'Do you think I fear you old man. My life is over already. I merely wish to take you with me. There, I free you of your bonds. Here is your own sword. Let us settle this once and for all!'

Owain shouted to his friends.'This will be between me and Zaba, do not use your powers to interfere, whatever happens.'

With this he stepped back. It felt good to have his gladius in his hands again, and be facing an opponent in the way he had since he first became an adult. However, he realised that the hours with his hands tied had left him a little stiff, and he knew he needed a few minutes to warm himself up. Zaba's blood was up however, and he was not likely to agree to any request. So be it, he would have to use the wiles learned in years of fighting in the arena to give himself a little time. Zaba advanced hard and fast, swinging his long cavalry sword with great sweeping blows. Owain merely parried them, they were almost laughably signalled by his body, Owain always knew what was coming next, and he retreated slowly whilst he regained his full mobility. Zaba was becoming infuriated by the ease in which Owain parried his blows with his much shorter sword.

Irritated too, by the smile that played on Owain's lips as he met each blow. Fit as he was, Zaba knew that this was taking all of his energy, at the cost of very little energy to the older man. Zaba only knew one way to fight, and he was used to rapid success, but this was different. He had heard of an old British fighting trick, where you feint a high blow and then aim for the legs, crippling your opponent, and ending the fight. He decided it was his best chance, and he raised the sword high for an apparent head blow then, with the sword in the air, changed his stance and the swing of the sword into a low, wide blow at the knees of Owain. The old gladiator had however, seen the trick coming a mile off, and he took another step back at the last moment. Zaba was left unbalanced and his side was totally exposed. With a speed of foot that would not have shamed a man one third his age, Owain stepped back in and stabbed at Zaba's exposed side with a short, powerful motion. As the sword went in deep, Owain twisted his wrist and withdrew. As the sword left Zaba's body, so did his life. Death was immediate.

Zaba's men gasped with horror, they had never seen him bested in a fight, a few more of them slipped off into the forest. It was Marcus who took the initiative now. He drew his own sword, and before the Druids could help, swung a huge blow that sent Owain's sword flying out of his hands. Quickly he advanced on a seemingly unarmed Owain. However, Owain still had the small dagger given to him by Branwen. It was hidden in the leather wristband he always wore. Retreating rapidly, to avoid the savage stabs made by Marcus' sword, he pulled the dagger from its hiding place, and as Marcus made another frantic assault, Owain stepped aside to avoid the thrust and stabbed the dagger low into Marcus' side. It was not a killing blow, but it was enough to incapacitate the spy. Bran pressed himself against a tree and threw his weapon aside, and shook his head indicating that he was no threat. But now the remains of Zaba's troop were advancing, bent on revenge, and Owain had only a short dagger for defence.

The atmosphere changed in a moment, as the air was rent by a bloodcurdling, bestial roar. The Batavians knew the sound immediately and yelled or whispered the same word 'Bear!' Bran, tending to Marcus, whispered that there were no bears in this part of Britain, nor had there been in living memory. As he spoke the great, grunting roar came again, and out of the forest at a speed that was impossible for a mere man, came Garth.

He was bare chested and he carried no weapons, but the roars coming from his throat were not human, they belonged to an adult male bear in a great rage. Some way behind him came Pered, Lorchar and Branwen, all fully armed. They could not keep up with the half human, half bear that was Garth. As he reached the first of the Batavians that rushed at him, weapons drawn, he merely flung them through the air as if they were made of straw. They landed on the forest floor with all the air driven out of their bodies. He was amongst the rest of the soldiers now, armed warriors all, but they stood no chance against this force of nature. Mere glancing blows knocked men unconscious, full on strikes crumpled up their bodies like men hit by chariots. Garth did receive a number of superficial wounds but they did not slow his speed or assuage his anger.

Eventually, not one of the cavalrymen was still on his feet and Garth stood side by side with his father, his great chest rising and falling as he was embraced by the weeping gladiator. Pered, Lorchar and Branwen moved among the injured soldiers. If they made to fight, they were ruthlessly dispatched, if they raised their hands in submission or were incapacitated, their weapons were taken from them. They were dragged to the horses and told to leave without delay.

Branwen took over from Bran and tended the wound in the spy's side. Marcus grunted with the pain as Branwen expertly, but none too tenderly, stitched up his wound, then applied a salve to prevent corruption of the wound.

'What in the name of all the Gods was that? I knew about Alwyn's power and had heard that you and the twins had, shall we say special abilities but I was led to believe that Owain's boy was no more than a very large, strong warrior, expertly taught by his father. But that was not like anything I have ever seen before. He looked like a man, but he had all the speed and power of a wild bear. Those were Batavian warriors that he cast aside like toys. By all accounts, his father was an exceptional gladiator, but what would Romans not pay to see him in the arena, if that bear power could be harnessed?'

Branwen finished her ministrations with a hiss of fury and gave a spiteful final rub of the wound that was harder than was strictly required, drawing a foul word from Marcus. The young healer laughed, though there was no mirth in her voice as she replied.

'You will never understand will you? You believe that everyone and every thing has a price. You see only opportunities for you to increase your wealth and power. There is a reason that some Druids have these powers, and seemingly no Roman does. These powers are not to be corrupted, they are for the general good and for serving the Truth. Those few like Maelgwyn who forget this are not able to grow their powers again and, if we were able to, as of old, he would long ago have been destroyed for his evil use of his powers. Garth was harnessing the spirit of the Bear, with which he has an affinity. The spirit was especially strong in him then, as he was able to use the fear of what might happen to his father, and his fury at those who took him. He would never be able or willing to bring out that power to give entertainment for the jaded tastes of the citizens of Rome. Look at what happened when we bested you today. Those who did not want to fight us were allowed to leave, and even you, the cause of Owain's capture and ill treatment, we did not kill you in cold blood, as we could have. I have even healed you first, though I have friends that need my care, because your need was the greatest. That is the way of the Truth.'

Marcus merely snarled his contempt 'And that, girl, is why, in the end we will be victorious and the power of Druids destroyed forever!'

Then the spy was aware of another close by him, he looked up and saw the slender form and cool, appraising blue eyes of Alwyn upon him. Alwyn spoke quietly but with some purpose.

'You may be right, Marcus the spy. It is true that the few of us with exceptional powers can do many things, but it seems unlikely that we can stop a legion of well armed and trained soldiers from destroying our comrades. You may indeed kill us all, but you cannot kill the Truth. It is the essence of our world, the circle of being. It exists in every tree and stream, lake, marsh, mountain and sea, and every creature in the world and there will always be those, like us, who are in tune with it. It would be a shame if all the knowledge of this Truth that we have learned over the centuries is lost, but the Truth itself will never die, as long as our world exists. It is our job to to try and maintain our knowledge of the Truth, and teach it to those who would learn. The Romans it seems, are hell bent on destroying us, but they cannot destroy the Truth'

Now it was Bran's turn to show his contempt. 'Mere words boy. They may sound well to uneducated peasants, or to those who do not understand how the world really operates. These words will achieve nothing however, in the face of those who have power and are prepared to wield it. Like the Romans and yes, like my master! You know that in the end he will either kill you or control you?'

Alwyn merely laughed, mirthlessly. 'And where is your vaunted master now? He is cowering in some cave in the mountains, hoping that I cannot reach him to hurt him again. As long as he keeps out of our affairs, he is safe, but I warn him now, through you, that the next time he tries to harm me or any of my friends, I shall regard it as self defence to use all my mental powers to hit back. I cannot tell if it will kill him, or merely leave him as one of those poor souls whose mothers have to feed them with a spoon though they have the body of a grown man. I believe his mother died of shame some years ago, so I hope you feel up to the task of caring for someone who has lost his mind for the rest of his, or your, life.'

With these withering words Alwyn turned on his heel and walked away. Now Owain arrived and gave Bran a powerful kick.

'On your feet lad and be on your way. You are unharmed, and you can take a horse and flee back to your master. By the way, do not make the mistake of regarding me as you would one of my young friends here. I have great respect for them, but I do not share all their beliefs. I would have no problem in killing you here and now, in ways more painful than you would believe, but I do not wish to upset my friends. However I tell you this now, as a fair warning . . .' At this point he seized the man by the throat with one hand and lifted him bodily off his feet, his face inches away from Bran's. '. . . If I ever see you again I will tear you limb from limb with these bare hands. Now, go and never let me see those cold eyes of yours again' With these words Owain released the white faced sputtering warrior who fell to the ground, before he rose quickly to his feet after another hard kick. He stumbled to the horses and rode quickly off without a backward glance.

Owain now turned his attention to Marcus. Branwen had finished her ministrations to him and had moved on to Garth, so the Roman spy was alone with the grizzled old gladiator.

'Now then Marcus, whatever your the rest of your name is. If I read you aright, you are already calculating how quickly you can get together a really unbeatable force of legionaries, so that you can either capture us or kill us. Either way, you get your revenge. Sadly we do not always get our way. If we did, I would now be killing you in a way that even you could not imagine. So . . . what will actually happen will be this. I tell you now, though you will remember nothing of it, so you can appreciate the full horror of it even while you deny that this could happen in the rational world of a Roman spy and would be politician. You will forget all of this, you will have no memory of these events and you will be totally unable to explain what has happened to sixty cavalrymen. When some of the survivors report back with ludicrous stories of strange forest happenings and men like bears, you will be unable to back them up. The Tribune of Cavalry will not be pleased with you. He may suspect that you are either drunk, or mad, or worse, part of some dreadful conspiracy. You may end up in military jail or perhaps even being tortured to tell what you know. But you will know nothing! Ah! I see from your face that you are sceptical. No matter! Let me introduce you to Cerna. She is going to sing you a lovely song, and soon you will forget all your worries. Then you will be put on a cavalry horse which will find its way back to its fort and then your real troubles will begin. Even if someone, Maelgwyn say, or Bran tries to tell you about Alwyn and the others, you will suffer such a violent headache that it will block out everything else. You will never remember these events.'

Then Marcus saw Cerna, she was young and undoubtedly lovely, she had a kind of unearthly quality to her that made Marcus smile, even in his state of abject fear. Then she began to sing. Ah! she sang such a sweet song that the spy quite forgot his problems, and lost himself in the lovely music. Eventually, he found himself on a horse, travelling slowly through the forest. He found he had no memory of why he was there or what had been happening. For a while this disturbed him, but soon he surrendered himself to the repetitive sound of the hose's hooves on the forest floor and ceased worrying about where he was and why.

Back in the glade in the wood the seven looked around at the scene of devastation around them. Lorchar spoke first. 'I have no doubt that the local people will come, bury the dead and spirit away any of the useful possessions. However, once again we have been forced to use our powers, here in the sacred forest to kill and wound those who would harm us. It would be good, I think, to perform a little ceremony to thank the spirits of the forest for their help, and to expiate a little of our crime against the peace of the forest. Branwen, it fell to you to make the greatest use of the spirits, and you are closest to them. Do you know what to do in order to set things right?'

'I believe I do Lorchar. Not far from here is a spring that wells up and feeds a stream. It would be a suitable place to perform an act of cleansing. Garth, Pered, you have both called upon the spirit of forest creatures to attain victory here, perhaps you would help me?'

With these words Branwen moved swiftly to the body of Zaba and removed a thick gold arm ring from him. Pered and Garth did likewise with two others of the dead, and the other four followed behind, as the front three, carrying their treasure, reverently moved through the forest to a deep dell, where clear water bubbled up into a small pool, that fed a stream, that ran down the hill. Branwen laid down the arm ring and promptly removed her clothes, quickly followed by Pered and Garth. The three of them waded into the pool and, taking the lead from Branwen raised the three pieces of gold high. In a clear, confident voice, Branwen spoke.

'Spirits of the forest, you have given us great aid today in our fight with those who seek to prevent us speaking of the Truth. However, in accomplishing our victory, we have spilt blood, yes, and killed in your sacred forest. For this we seek your forgiveness. To show that we have done these deeds not for our own gain but in support of the Truth, we give to you these baubles of gold that men covet, but which we know are nothing, compared to the Truth. But more, we pledge to you that we will always seek the Truth and never use the powers you grant to us for any other purpose.'

With these words first Branwen then Pered and finally Garth tossed their pieces of gold into the deepest part of the pool before each of them began a process of ritual washing. Cerna and Lorchar, watching from above, commenced a haunting chant until the ritual was complete, and the three emerged from the pool and dressed again. There was silence for a few moments, eventually broken by Owain.

'Come, my friends we need to put a few miles between us and that place of death up there. The Garrison will send out scouts to discover what has happened by early light tomorrow'

They returned to their horses and rode off to the west. Keeping up a good steady pace for several hours before Owain, whose old bones ached more than anyone else's, called a halt for the day.

'Well I expect you are all exhausted and hungry by now, and this place looks as good as any so here we will camp and make some food and spend the night before we continue with our journey. Branwen, my dear, can you go into the forest and forage for us. All we have is oatmeal and some honey and I know these young men in particular will appreciate some meat, roots and herbs to make their meal more palatable'

Branwen, grinned her cheekiest grin back at him. 'Aye Lord Owain, and shall I bring some willow bark for those who are feeling the pain of travel the most?'

'I really do not know whom you are speaking of, young woman.' replied Owain with false haughtiness that brought roars of laughter all round.

Soon camp was prepared and a fire lit. a pan was filled with water and oatmeal and salt added. Everyone sat round with warm cloaks or blankets wrapped around them. Branwen then appeared back in camp with three fat hares already skinned and chopped and a number of herbs and washed roots to add to the pot. She also had a quantity of willow bark which she steeped in a small pot of water to make a tisane for Owain. The old warrior gave a satisfied groan as he sat back and sipped the tisane, which he noted was flavoured with honey and wild mint. Branwen produced a small container from her pack in which was a salve which she rubbed into Owain's sore knees and ankles. The salve produced an agreeable warmth which seemed to ease his aches. He turned down the offer of some more of the salve for his back and the soon the seven were sitting round the camp fire, replete from their meal and discussing the day's events.

It was Lorchar who spoke first. 'When the Romans learn of the loss of their troop, they will not know what to make of it, but they will send in their forces to try to find out. We still have the main part our mission to accomplsh. We have the Torc of Aneurin. However we still need King Bran's Cauldron and we need to take both of them to Erin for safe keeping. So we must return to Avalon and quickly, seek the Cauldron from Eirlys and secure passage to Erin. We must do all of this before the Romans know of us. So in my opinion we must set off at once to seek the Lady Eirlys, without delay'

Owain groaned, though he knew the that Lorchar, spoke only common sense. 'Very well, if we must, Garth my boy, you have the wounds of battle, are you up to the journey?

Garth grinned that characteristic open smile that caused Cerna's heart to melt. "Father I am quite recovered. Branwen's medical skills are excellent, and you know I believe that I still have some of the spirit of the bear running through me, because now I have eaten and rested a little, I feel even stronger than usual.'

Owain painfully heaved himself to his feet, stretched his back and sighed 'On we go then my friends, it will not take us too long to return to Avalon. Alwyn, I take it that the Lady Eirlys is already aware of the events of the day?'

'She is, Owain and she is arranging for local people to clear away the bodies, weapons and remains of the camp. By the time we get back to Avalon she will have made arrangements for our ongoing journey. She is delighted that you are well, but concerned that the Romans will seek indiscriminate revenge for the loss of their troop.

Owain shook his head with wonder. 'I will never get used to this world that I cannot see or hear going on around me. If there were more that had your powers the Romans would never have succeeded in invading at all!

However Eirlys is right to be concerned about the Roman response to this loss. The local Tribune will not believe the tales of enchantment and invisible forces that survivors take back, but he will not take kindly to the defeat and destruction of a troop of Batavians. The local people for some miles around should hide any weapons they have and feign total ignorance, but there will, I am afraid, be an increase in Roman patrols and the treatment of people will be brutal and cruel, as the Romans seek to re-establish their aura of fear and invincibility. I suspect that many around here will come to resent the Roman presence even more than they do already'

The travellers set off on their long ride back to Avalon. Alwyn spurred his pony on and rode alongside Branwen, to her great delight. After a few minutes silence, Alwyn spoke.

'I did not have the chance to tell you earlier Branwen, but I was very impressed with the way that you dealt with the situation back at the Batavian camp. Of course I already knew you were very brave, fearless really, but the calm way you thought things through and kept Owain safe whilst on your own in the midst of the enemy was a revelation, even to me. One thing puzzles me though Branwen. I know you to be the kindest and most caring person in our group, yet somehow, when the time comes, you are able to transform yourself into a fierce killer. I have found the killing the hardest thing to come to terms with, yet you, the youngest of us with no background in combat like Owain, Garth and even Lorchar, have taken to it with ease. How can that be?'

Branwen gave Alwyn a sharp, appraising look, checking that there was no hint of criticism or distaste in his question. She saw the cool blue eyes, open and curious, with only a hint of concern on his kind face and she breathed a sigh of relief before replying.

'What you forget Alwyn, when you speak of my youth and kindness and my lack of combat experience, is that I am no novice at killing. I have lived in the forest since infancy, and I learned to kill what I needed to eat at a very young age. My mother taught me to respect the creatures of the forest, but showed me how to regard them in the way they regard each other. So, if we wished to eat meat, we needed to understand that the cost of that was the death of a living creature. The difference between us and them is that we should only kill when we had to and then we should seek forgiveness from spirit of the creatures we killed.'

'If it seemed to you that I took joy in the killing of men, that was not the case. it seems that when I have to kill, man or beast I can only really do it when it is necessary. When I was a young child, I once killed a mouse, simply because I could. My mother chided me for it, and indeed I felt the pain of it for some time after. It was only when my mother showed me how to pray for forgiveness to the forest spirits that I could gain any peace. I will not deny that the excitement and danger of a fight rouses me, but do not mistake it, I am always in control, always checking that if I have to kill, it is truly justified by need. I know it has been harder for you, with the more sheltered upbringing of the Druids' school, but it seems to me that you have taken to it very well. The way you planned the tactics for the fight against the Batavians could hardly have been bettered by Owain, indeed he told me that himself,' at this point, her excited young face steadied and grew serious. 'Alwyn, even I can see that you are the most special of us all. Not so much for your powers, we all have amazing gifts in that way. No it is your mind and spirit that make you special. In many ways you represent what we are seeking to do on this quest. You must know that I . . . that is we, would all sacrifice ourselves to save you'

Branwen's voice cracked and failed at this point and she looked away so that Alwyn would not see the tears in her eyes. When she turned back with a loud sniff, she found, to her amazement, that Alwyn's eyes too were full of tears, though his face wore a broad smile.

'You know' he breathed, 'I do believe that we would all gladly sacrifice ourselves to save any one of us. And as to which of us is most vital to our quest, what about you? There is only ever one Lady of the Flowers in all the world and you are that one, Branwen, you are special to us all and to me more than anyone' He flushed as he said these words, gripped Branwen's hand and then turned his pony aside to return to Owain. Branwen's spirits soared at these words and she had to restrain herself as flowers were spontaneously appearing on the trees and shrubs she rode past.

Chapter 13

They slept that night in a quiet woodland glade and after breaking their fast set off again down the track to the west. After an hour or so Alwyn rode up to Owain and spoke quietly and urgently to him.

"Owain, up ahead we are approaching a Roman patrol. Regular cavalry I think, as their thoughts are in Latin which I understand well. They are unaware of yesterday's fight. I think it is a regular patrol looking for armed Britons. What will they make of our weapons? Will we have to fight again?'

Owain shrugged, then smiled at the worried face of the young Druid.

'Well, we must make the best of the situation. No point in trying to run off and hide, that might excite greater suspicion later. I have a few secrets up my sleeve, that, with luck, will get us out of this without a fight, or the need to make more open use of your powers. But ride at the front with Garth and me, and see what you make of the situation with your greater perception. First, however ride back and warn the others about the situation. I will speak to Garth.'

Alwyn quickly did as he was bid with a glow of pride in his heart at what he perceived as a real expression of Owain's trust in his powers and intelligence. Garth was up at Owain's side after his father gave him an almost imperceptible signal.

Owain spoke quickly and quietly to his son. 'My boy, Alwyn tells me that we are about to run into a Roman patrol, regular cavalry apparently, so your first encounter with real Roman military. All may be well, but leave all the talking to me, show no surprise at anything I say, and use your experience to watch the eyes and expressions of the soldiers. We will have Alwyn alongside, but your trained warrior's instinct may be even quicker and more certain than his powers. I trust you absolutely, and you will know if and when we have to fight for our lives and the safety of our charges.'

Garth merely smiled grimly and nodded, but his heart was filled with pride at his father's trust in him. Next, Owain called Branwen to his side.

"Branwen my dear, we are about to meet with Roman soldiery, I do not believe we have a great deal to fear, but just in case I want you to tie your pony to Lorchar's and then perform your disappearing trick. Move alongside of us and stay invisible as we meet the Romans. If the worst comes to worst and fighting begins, it will be your duty to protect Alwyn by whatever means you have at your disposal. Is that clear?'

Branwen nodded, her eyes shining with pride and her face flushed. She dropped back and conferred swiftly with Lorchar. As Branwen disappeared from view, Lorchar trotted up to Owain and spoke quietly with him.

"So Owain, I take it we are putting in to operation the plan we agreed some time ago?'

Owain, tight lipped, nodded agreement. 'That is so. Will you go back and ensure that Cerna is well protected and that Pered keeps his head?'

Lorchar gave Owain a swift sharp smile of reassurance and moved back to talk urgently with the twins while Alwyn and Garth moved up either side of Owain.

Within a few minutes the travellers came in sight of the Roman Cavalry detachment of about twenty men with an Optio leading the column. As soon as the Romans saw the party appear round the bend, the first eight soldiers moved up alongside their officer and the men behind took up swift defensive positions. Owain led his small party onward at the same unhurried pace, until ordered to halt in the Optio's broken British. Owain raised his hand, stopped his party and gave the Roman officer a calm greeting in his perfect, Roman accented Latin. "Salve, Optio. What can we do for you this morning?'

To his credit, the officer made a decent fist at hiding his amazement at being greeted by Briton who spoke perfect Latin in this western backwater, and one who showed surprisingly little fear for a man accompanied only by two women and three youths, even if one of them was immense and well armed.

He replied to Owain in Latin. 'May I compliment you sir, on your excellent Latin. However I must inform you that our mission is to ensure that none of the natives around here are armed with weapons of war. When we find them we are to confiscate them."

Owain seemed nonplussed. 'Excellent, Optio, a wise and sensible move, however, if there is nothing else, we have a long way to travel today, so perhaps you could let us pass'

There was a good deal of muttering from the cavalrymen at this perceived impudence, but the Optio merely ground his teeth and maintained the same stilted politeness that had characterised the early part of this exchange. 'Cannot help but notice, sir, that you and the large youth by your side are extremely well armed. Despite your excellent Latin, your dress and presence here would suggest that you are British, so I must insist that you hand over your weapons immediately, or face some truly unacceptable consequences"

Owain smiled indulgently at the young officer. 'My boy, I commend you on your politeness and your insistence on what you see as your duty. However, if you will permit an old soldier the licence to advise you, you should never judge purely by appearance. I take it these rules about weapons do not apply to Roman Citizens?

The young officer looked flustered and somewhat annoyed at being made to look foolish in front of his men, so it was with some asperity that he replied. 'Indeed not sir, but I hardly think that you . . . .'

Owain jumped in again with a broad smile on his lips, 'Tut! there you go again. It so happens that I am a Roman Citizen. Perhaps you would care to look at this."

With this, he produced from the folds of his cloak an embossed leather scroll case. He handed it over to the cavalry officer, who took it with a puzzled frown. The young soldier opened the case and drew out a yellowed vellum scroll with an opened seal attached. As he read from the scroll his eyebrows raised an a look of frank astonishment crept over his face.

"Sir, it says here that you are are a freeman and full Roman citizen and that you were granted your manumission and citizenship over twenty years ago by the then Emperor himself! It further states that you were granted these liberties as a reward for your long and distinguished service as a Gladiator. Sir, from your name, am I to assume that you are Owain the Briton? These last words were pronounced with a degree of awe that surprised most of his troop as well as the party of Druids.

Owain gave a small, but elegant bow. "At your service Optio. Though I must say I am surprised that you have heard of me. You must have been a mere infant when I reached the end of my career?'

'Indeed I was sir' the Optio replied breathlessly, 'but my father, we lived in Rome at the time, was a huge lover of the gladitorial contests and he always talked about you. He said you were the best there was. Never defeated in all those years. You were, well, a kind of hero to him. If he still lived he would be most pleased to hear of our meeting"

Owain bowed again, "You are too kind, young man. I am sorry to hear of the loss of you father. But yes, I am that old gladiator, now a Roman Citizen, though resident of Britain once again. So, I am entitled to bear arms, as is my son, Garth beside me. That lady behind me is my wife and these other young people are my adopted children, so all are entitled to the rights and liberties of a Roman Citizen"

The Optio pursed his lips, 'Indeed so sir. Perhaps you would be kind enough to tell me what such an exalted figure as yourself is doing riding around this land at the edge of the Empire with only your family with you.?'

Owain spread his arms wide. "Well you know, the island of Britain is my home and I have lived here ever since I left Rome. For many years I earned my keep as a trainer of warriors. But in truth, I am getting a little long in the tooth for that now, and the the Roman peace means there is little enough call for my services. So of late I have taken to travelling the roads. My lad and I give a few demonstration bouts, and he takes on any young man who fancies his chances in a fight and then my young adopted children here, are skilled and talented performers in some of the traditional British forms of music, song and story telling, so we find ourselves welcome wherever we roam. Of course this far west there are still a few lawless people on the roads, so we do need our weapons.'

This seemed to satisfy the Optio, who nodded and began to get his men back into column. Alwyn sharp eyes and mental perception picked up a different feeling from the soldier on the Optio's right hand. His face gave away his suspicion of Owain's story and he was surveying the whole group with hard eyes. Alwyn entered the cavalryman's mind gently and probed his thoughts. It was soon apparent that he thought these travellers were getting away too easily. His eyes fell on the empty saddle of Branwen's pony and he wondered whether there was another member of the group hiding nearby, and why. Then the man's eyes fell on Cerna and he wondered what a beauty like that would fetch at the slave market. As he thought this, Cerna's eyes rose in alarm as she picked up the sense of what the man was thinking. The soldier noticed this and was intrigued. He decided not to tell the Optio, who tended to play things according to regulation. He knew there were a few old hands like him in the troop, and that night when they were at camp, they would sneak away, come back, find this group of impudent natives, kill the men and boys and take the women as slaves. He would make up some story to satisfy the Tribune, putting the young Optio in a bad light as well. All these plans were now clear to Alwyn, and he was alarmed. He decided to act, without consulting Owain and Lorchar. His plan meant putting Branwen at some risk, but he was sure that she could handle it.

He sought out Branwen in his mind and passed his concerns to her. Through her thoughts Branwen replied 'I was worried about that one too. I never liked his eyes, or his expression, full of contempt for us. He must not be allowed to get to camp tonight, yet we must not alarm the others. Leave it to me, I think I have a plan'

'Very well Branwen, but you must be careful. If you cannot safely put your plan in operation, give it up and we will make preparations to deal with a group of them if they should attack!' Branwen could feel the concern in Alwyn's thoughts, and unseen, she grinned to herself

The Roman column was now moving off at a steady walk. Before following, Branwen checked the little bag she always carried on her belt. She pulled out a little oiled cloth package containing a small amount of a sticky black substance and nodded to herself. She loped after the Roman column, stopping momentarily to pick a few extra long thorns from a Blackthorn bush.

Branwen soon caught up with the slowly moving column. Moving alongside the soldier who harboured her friends such ill will, she concentrated deeply and caused an adder to appear in front of the horse's hooves. The beast reared up in fright and the cavalryman, although very skilled, was unable to stay on the horse, he tumbled in a heap onto the ground. In the confusion this caused in the column, Branwen, invisible to all the Romans, moved in and swiftly stuck the long thorn, coated with the black substance, into the thigh of the Roman soldier. He barely felt the thorn with the pain and embarrassment of the fall, and he quickly got to his feet and seized the reins of his horse. By now, the Optio had dropped back to discover the cause of the commotion and asked the man if he was alright. The soldier, red with shame at having fallen from his horse when at a walk replied brusquely that he was fine, and clambered back into the saddle. However, just as the column was getting itself into order to continue with their patrol, the soldier slumped forward against the horse's neck and slid heavily to the floor. Branwen allowed herself a slight smile. She knew that the amount of drug on that thorn should have the cavalryman unconscious for about 48 hours. Afterwards he would be fine and no-one, she was confident, would have the skill to discover what had been wrong with him. It would be put down to a heavy fall. Leaving the confused scene behind her Branwen swiftly ran back to join the others. Alwyn would, she was sure, be delighted with her work.

As she approached the others, she saw, to her surprise, Owain speaking very sternly to Alwyn, who was red faced and clearly upset. Suddenly, her arms were gripped by the lean brown hands of Lorchar, who hugged her in a way which showed she had been worried about her young protege.

'Branwen my dear, you are safe, thank the Gods!' she gasped with some emotion. 'We were so worried that the Romans would catch you. We were about to send Pered to check you were alright'

Despite being glad that Lorchar cared so deeply, Branwen was bristling at this statement, which she saw as a lack of confidence in her abilities.

'Surely, you knew that in these woods, not only am I invisible, but my power over nature would mean that I was never in any danger from those slow witted soldiers? Have I not done enough of late to give you belief in my intelligence and ability to think under pressure, as well as my powers to know I could look after myself?

By now the others had all gathered round and Owain shook his great grizzled head. 'Branwen my dear, you are a wonder, but Alwyn should never have sent you alone. Your powers and even your wit and common sense are not in doubt, however, you have much to learn about soldiers. You were invisible to the men, yes, but the horses would have been aware of your presence and cavalrymen are very sensitive to the behaviour of their horses. You could have been detected and killed!'

Branwen was furious 'I was not sent by Alwyn, as you so insultingly put it. He told me, with his mental powers, what the problem was, and I let him know that I knew how to deal with it, and I have. I am sorry to say this, Owain, because I respect and love you, but you have no idea of the extent of my powers, and so, skilled though you are in the fighting arts, you cannot really imagine how I can deal with a situation."

Alwyn stepped in at this point, anxious as always to keep the cohesion of their little group. 'Branwen is right in that, Owain, and I must say that it was unfair of you to accuse me of not caring what happened to Branwen. Actually I care very much what happens to her.' He coloured a little at this but acknowledged the huge smile Branwen fired at him. 'I will accept this aspect of your criticism however, I should have waited a few minutes to tell you all what I had learned so that we could have made a joint decision'

Owain was silent for a moment as he thought about what had been said. He glanced at Lorchar, who seemed to sense what he was thinking, and gave him an almost imperceptible nod, before he responded to what Alwyn and Branwen had said.

'Very well then, I accept the criticism that I am a little hidebound by my old fashioned views and my lack of understanding of the full range of your powers. I am glad you acknowledge that you should have discussed things before acting, and I am sorry if my hasty words, that came out of only my love and concern for Branwen's safety, have caused you two any pain.

To conclude the truce he clapped a massive hand on Alwyn's shoulder, which caused the young man's knees to buckle, and then scooped up Branwen with one mighty arm, hugging her to him until the laughing girl complained that he was crushing the air out of her lungs. This broke the tension and soon the group was on its way again, the younger ones gathering around Branwen as she told them how she had dealt with the Roman. Lorchar made a point of riding up alongside Owain and with a gentle touch on his arm and a sympathetic smile, she acknowledged the gesture Owain had made for the sake of harmony in the group.

Chapter 14

Early the next morning, just as the group were about to break camp, Alwyn warned Owain that people were approaching, but the smile on his face indicated that he knew they were not strangers. The little band made ready to meet their visitors and were delighted to see Lady Eirlys and Prince Tai leading a small band of mounted spearmen. When they dismounted Lorchar embraced Eirlys and Prince Tai and Garth shook hands warmly, as friendships had been forged in the few days the Druids had stayed at Avalon. They all sat round the newly revived camp fire and the news of recent days' events was exchanged.

Eirlys' face showed that she was concerned, both about the death and disruption at the camp of the Batavians and about the patrol of Roman cavalry. She voiced her concerns.

'Eventually the truth of what happened at the Batavian camp will emerge, though it might take a while to be believed. Somewhere a commander will put that alongside the report of the Roman regulars and conclusions will be arrived at that do not augur well for you my friends. I fear that already they look at the lands of the Dubonni and see them as part of the Empire proper. and that would make things difficult for us all. However, one thing is clear, you must leave these lands, and soon. Down at the cost, a few hours from here a vessel is waiting to leave for Erin, which

I believe is your next destination anyway. We will see that you get to that vessel in good time my friends'

Alwyn broke into the excited discussion with a hesitant voice. 'Lady Eirlys, Prince Tai, we are delighted at these arrangements, but, after all you have done I hardly know how to broach this, but Lord Myrthin charged us to . . .'

Eirlys smiled as she interrupted the young Druid. 'We know, he wanted you to take King Bran's Cauldron to Erin, so that it does not fall into the hands of the Romans. This is a hard thing to ask of us. It is the greatest treasure of Avalon and has been in our hands for generations. Prince Tai has spoken to his father the King and they are both agreed that to have it fall into the hands of the Romans and through them perhaps into the control of a turncoat like Maelgwyn would be the worst of all outcomes. So . . .'

With these words she turned and pulled from a leather bag a small bronze cauldron of antique design, covered with beautiful figures dancing and fighting. Reverently, Alwyn took it from her hands and held it up for the others to see. Owain sniffed.

"Well it is a pretty enough little piece but only bronze, it is old I understand but surely it cannot be . . .'

Before he had finished his words, Eirlys had interjected. 'This cauldron in the right hands could be the most powerful tool you have bring the Truth to the people of Britain once again. In the wrong hands it could destroy our culture forever. It has certain properties that I expect you will be sceptical of Owain, but believe me I expect that young Alwyn here will be able to use it in a way that should bring you to a new level of belief in the powers and spirits that underly the Truth'

Alwyn, seemingly entranced by the ancient object, spoke hesitantly again. 'May we . . . you know, try it out? Whilst you are here to advise us? I should hate us to look uncertain and clumsy when we come before the Kings and Druids of Erin.'

Eirlys smiled gently at Alwyn and looked round to see the bright shining eyes of Cerna and Branwen, the attempt by Pered to look cooly indifferent, belied by the way he licked his lips anxiously, and the frank puzzlement on the faces of Owain and Garth. She glanced at Lorchar, who flashed a short, nervous smile and nodded quickly her agreement.

'Very well then, fetch the items we need.' These words were spoken to her servant who rushed off and returned quickly with a bag containing sealed pots. Eirlys selected one large pot and one tiny vial. From the large pot she poured a clear liquid with a strange smell into the Cauldron. Then she opened the vial and carefully allowed one thick, viscous drop to fall in the clear liquid.

Instantly, there was a reaction. The liquid steamed and hissed, and briefly an acrid smell made those nearest to the Cauldron cough. Then the liquid in the bowl settled. It was now blacker than any substance they had ever seen, and its surface still and dense but somehow more reflective than the finest silver mirror. Lorchar and Eirlys shut their eyes and stretched out their hands over the surface of the liquid. Together they began a soft, rhythmic incantation in an ancient version of the British tongue. Owain glaced at Pered and saw that he was repeating the words of the incantation to himself, memorising them as only a trained Bard can.

Meanwhile Alwyn, Cerna and Branwen, holding hands leant over the Cauldron and rocked back and fro to the rhythm of the incantation of the older Druids. At first they could see nothing but the reflection of the leaves on the trees above the cauldron, but slowly, first to Alwyn, then to Cerna and faintly to Branwen pictures started to appear. They saw a small ship on a grey sea. They saw another ship, with oars, draw near, they heard shouts and screams, they saw arrows and spears fly. Then they saw the other ship draw swiftly away and return the way it had come. Finally they saw a pale beach and behind it a headland of green grass and grey rocks. On the headland were many men. Two of them hand circelets of gold on their heads and and the finest armour. Five more were in the dark green robes of the Druids of Erin and they had narrow circlets of shining bronze round their heads. Behind were many spearmen but all were raising their hands in greeting and smiling broadly. As Alwyn saw this image he stetched out his hands over the Cauldron and raised them slowly over his head. As he hid so a fine mist lifted from the surface of the Cauldron and seemed to hover a few feet in the air. Slowly this mist resolved itself into an almost solid three dimensional version of the final image, but as though seen through a slight fog. Every person in that glade could see this image and many sank to their knees in fear of this new expression of the powers of the Druids. Even Owain could feel his mouth drying and the hairs on the back of his neck standing on end. He could not explain what he just seen, but he knew it for what it was.

'So then, we are to arrive safe in Erin and receive a welcome from Kings and Druid'

Unexpectedly, Lochar, normally the calmest of people, seemed consumed with anger and frustration at this simple statement.

'Owain, you are not a fool, after these last few weeks experiences, can you not comprehend the scale of what you have just witnessed? The Lady Eirlys here is one of the most respected and powerful Druids in Britain, and yet she could not have accomplished the act you have just seen. I myself, am a Mona trained Druid of some twenty years experience, with what are considered to be great powers, and yet I could not begin to do what three young Druids, two of them with only a month as Druids, have accomplished. No living person has seen a Druid accomplish what Alwyn did on his first acquaintance with the Cauldron, namely to make what he sees in the Cauldron manifest for others. These three have performed wonders and you seem to regard it as no more than hearing a message delivered on the road!'

Before the astonished Owain could respond, Eirlys stepped in and calmed the situation. 'Lorchar my dear, remember that barely a month ago Owain believed in none of our powers, and now he accepts as a fact, something that a few weeks ago he would have dismissed as a conjuring trick. You cannot expect him to understand how important and historic what we have seen here today really is! However, I would warn all of you to beware of reading too much into predictions of the future. What you have seen will come to pass. But there is so much we do not know. When will that happen? Were those Kings and Druids of Erin really welcoming or just pretending to and do all of you survive the journey? Alwyn, what else did you see that you did not show to the rest of us?'

Alwyn showed a puzzled face before he hesitantly replied. 'It would seem that on this journey we are attacked, I would guess by pirates from Erin. The Cauldron showed us drive the attackers away, but arrows and spears rained on our ship for a short while. Who knows who might be injured, or even killed before the pirates draw off?. I find that I cannot read minds of people in events that have not yet happened. Cerna, were you able to draw any other information from what we saw?'

'I can say that the kings and Druids of Erin are pleased to welcome us. I was able to read that emotion strongly.' Cerna hesitated here, her green eyes filled with tears as she went on. 'However I felt pain and terror during the pirate attack. I believe that someone I care about, that of course includes all of you, is at least hurt in that attack. I . . . I cannot tell if anyone dies!'

Cerna bent her head and began sobbing here. Before even Garth and Pered could move to comfort her, Branwen was at her side, her arm around Cerna's shoulders, spirited as ever, she made her contribution to the story.

'As you know my powers as a seer are more limited than Alwyn's or Cerna's, but sometimes, I am permitted to see things others do not. We drive the pirates away with our combined powers and the warlike appearance of Owain and Garth. They do not expect to see fully armed, fearsome warriors on our little ship! I believe no-one does die, but I think it will be a close run thing and I cannot tell who it will be."

Owain now had resumed his role as the straight talking, bluff soldier. 'So be it! We are better prepared than most are in such a situation. Would that I had always been forearmed before a battle. Eirlys I thank you for all your help, and I apologise to you and Lorchar and these young people for my crassness in not seeing the significance of today's revelations. As you so rightly say until recently I believed in none of this and now, each day I find my preconceptions and ideas challenged in a way I never expected at my time of life. I see now what an amazing tool this little Cauldron could be for spreading the Truth and what a terrible weapon it could be in the hands of the Romans and Maelgwyn. Shall we break camp now and head for the coast to prepare for our journey to Erin.

Chapter 15

A few hours later the travellers were loading their belongings from the muddy banks of a creek into one of the tiny ships that hugged the coasts of the Havren Sea before risking the stormy channel across to Erin. The tough, weather beaten sailors, with their short swords and bows in weather proof cases looked like they were used to dealing with pirate attacks but still Prince Tai was fretting that he was sending his friends off to face a dangerous situation without extra help.

'The captain tells me he cannot take any of my soldiers for added protection, and I can see that there is in truth, little room. What I can do is give you some extra shields, large ones made of weathered hide, they will help keep the pirate arrows from harming our precious young friends."

Owain smiled and shook the hand of the handsome young Prince as he accepted the offer of the shields. Eirlys was making the rounds of the the young Druids and many tears were being shed. Owain gruffly cut the goodbyes short after he caught the anxious glances of the captain checking the tide. 'Come my friends our seafaring companions here wish to be away before we lose the tide and the evening breeze. Finish your goodbyes and let us complete the wishes of our beloved Myrthin and get our precious cargo to Erin'

All packed aboard the crew skillfully cast off and used the tide and a stern oar to navigate out of the creek and raised the sail as they entered the rougher waters of the great Havren estuary. The little ship hugged the coastline, avoiding sandbanks and rocks with great skill. A few hours later as it became dark they dropped anchor in a little deserted bay, sleeping around a campfire on the beach with three men taking turns to keep watch. Their journey continued like this for three more days and nights until at last they could see ahead of them the open sea. Owain moved up close to the captain and spoke quietly to him. 'Does this mean that we have given the pirates the slip this time?'

The Captain, a taciturn man with a heavily scarred face that spoke of many meetings with pirates grimaced and spat.

'I wish it did, my Lord, they could be lying in wait behind one of the little islands here about, or they could come out from one of the rivers on the coast of Erin itself. They have men out watching the coast so we would be lucky if we did not encounter them. Indeed this stretch here is one of the most risky, so it would be as well for you and your son to don your armour and take up your weapons and get your young Druids protected behind those great shields of Prince Tai. If they have have half the powers I hear of them, they should bring them to bear as soon as they can'

Owain did as he was bid, not without some protests from the ever headstrong Pered who could not bear to be treated as some precious, delicate cargo. However the advice was sound for within an hour, Alwyn was shouting that the pirates were on their way, and indicated the direction of their approach, though the sharp eyed seamen could see nothing as yet. Owain prevailed upon them to take Alwyn's words seriously and bows, arrows and spears were taken from their weather proof casings. All of this was just in time for soon the watching seamen saw the long, low, leather boat propelled swiftly over the waves by numerous oarsmen, and the coarse yells of the pirates, intended to unsettle travellers. As the pirates drew near they were somewhat amazed to see two large, well armed and amoured warriors waving great spears and hurling imprecations back at them. They were surprised at the line of silent sailors, each with drawn bows, and they were decidedly unsettled by the sight of a woman Druid in the Black robes of Mona screaming detailed and frightening curses at them in their own tongue.

Their leader, a giant of a man with a metal cap and long red beard was made of sterner stuff however and drove them on with fierce words and threats of his own. soon the first pirate arrows thudded into the wooden side of the little ship and the great shields at one end. Behind those shields the young Druids were using their powers to increase the fear and confusion in the minds of the their attackers. Cerna was singing a song of drowning to the pirates in their own tongue, describing the horrors of that death in shocking detail. Pered was bellowing words of power that had hardened pirates vomiting over the sides of their boat. Branwen was screaming curses that set the teeth of the pirates on edge and turned more than one man's bowels to water. Alwyn, as usual was silent, picking out the minds of the most frightened, and filling those minds with disturbing images that had several throw themselves in the water with terror. The pirate leader could not understand what was happening, and in his fury he hurled a great spear at Owain who simply stepped aside from it. Unfortunately it flew on and actually penetrated the shield that protected Cerna. The young Druid was shocked, though unharmed, but the incident threw Pered into one of his incontrollable rages. He threw his shield aside and with an angry roar seized his great boar spear, a weapon unsuitable for throwing and hurled it with all the speed and might he could muster at the pirate boat. By sheer luck or by the guidance of a provident spirit the huge spear flew with unerring accuracy at the unprotected chest of the pirate leader. It penetrated right through his massive torso and sent him flying over the side. This was the last straw for the by now terrified pirates who were convinced they had attacked a spirit ship, and they turned and sped off back to the coast pursued by a score of arrows. Seamen, warriors and Druids alike gave a great shout of triumph and were still excitedly discussing their victory when they heard the shouts of Cerna and Branwen who were on their knees tending to a bleeding and wounded Pered, who had a black arrow sticking in his thigh. In the last assault of the pirates a stray arrow had caught the young Druid. Cerna cradled her brother's head and sang a song that took away his pain as

Branwen, using a small knife, skilfully removed the arrow, applied ointments and dressed the wound. She then looked at the arrow with a worried face and got up gesturing to Owain and Alwyn to join her. In a quiet voice she spoke to her two friends.

'Smell this arrow head' she brusquely demanded. Alwyn could make nothing of the strange sour smell, but Owain immediately recognised it as poison, and cursed the pirates accordingly. Branwen nodded 'Yes, it is poison Owain, a strong, plant based poison, one I could easily counter if I was in the midst of my beloved forest. But here, on a ship, I am limited. I do have some power of healing in my hands but I doubt it is sufficient to counter this poison. He will not last to Erin if I do not do something. I have one idea. Alwyn, the Torc of Aneurin that you wear today, as I understand it amplifies your own power? Well maybe it will do the same for me. Give it to me to try and see if it can amplify my power of healing to save Pered'

Both Branwen and Owain were astonished that Alwyn hesitated, he seemed reluctant to hand over the Torc. Owain spoke sharply and with some force. 'Hand the thing over Alwyn, for pity's sake, the Torc is just a bauble with some special powers, it must be used for good or else it is just a clumsy lump of gold!'

Owain's words seemed to break Alwyn's trance and rather shamefacedly he handed Branwen the great Torc. It was loose around her slender neck so she tightened it an immediately felt the power of it coursing through her whole body. She knelt down to Pered and placed her hands on the arrow wound. She muttered various prayers and incantations whilst Cerna held her brother's head and keened out her own powerful prayers. After a few moments of this Cerna looked up in astonishment at Branwen, as her power, amplified by the Torc worked its wonders on her brother and Cerna could feel the power coursing through Pered and making her hands and arms tingle and grow stronger as well. In a few minutes Pered was awake and smiling. Branwen slowly removed the Torc from her neck and with a curious expression on her face was handing it back to Alwyn when Lorchar stepped forward and grabbed it herself.

'I think I had better take charge of that for now, for none of you properly understand just how powerful an artefact this is. Myrthin warned me about the Torc. Did you never wonder why such a powerful tool for Druids would be hidden away, far from Mona? For generations Head Druids have passed the Torc to trusted friends, so that it could be kept from those who would misuse its power. Can you imagine what someone like Maelgwyn could do with this?'

Branwen dared to interrupt 'Lorchar, I felt something of what I can only call its wrongness just now. I could not understand why I felt this, because I was doing good according to the Truth, yet I felt a kind of encircling coldness, alongside a seductive awareness of how powerful the Torc made me.'

Cerna nodded her agreement 'I too felt that coldness, though I was not wearing the Torc. The shocking thing is, even though Branwen was saving my brother using powers I do not possess, I wanted to snatch the Torc from her neck and put it on myself. Its power was coming through my brother's body into my hands as I held his head'

Everyone now turned to Alwyn who looked a little shame faced. 'On each of the three times I used the Torc I was so wrapped up with the crisis we were dealing with that I confess I missed these signs of what damage the Torc can do to the Truth. Only just now when I found myself reluctant to hand it over to Branwen, did I realise there was something wrong. I was becoming all too fond of the great power it gave me. Lorchar, from what you have been told why is such a powerful tool for good turning us aside from the Truth?

Lorchar took a deep breath before replying. 'Well, I do not know the full story, but Myrthin told me this. Before we came to these lands another race lived here, no, not the ancestor folk, another race that ruled them. They were a powerful and adept priest class like us, but prepared to use any form of power to retain their grip on the people. Gradually our people, with their use of metal and horses defeated these older ones, the early Druids like Aneurin, were prepared to work with this older priest class and learn some of their skills and in return taught them about metals and other powers. Aneurin, and the Chief Priest of the old ones became friends and together they made this Torc. You see it has nine strands of gold intertwined. That is because the Torc increases the powers of the adept nine fold. However the Chief Priest did not tell Aneurin that he had woven into the torc, spirit powers that do not accord with our understanding of the Truth, spirits of dead priests of the old ones. These spirits are greedy for renewed life and in time, if someone became too fond of using the Torc they could live again in the body of that person. Aneurin was almost lost to these spirits before he saw the danger and hurled the Torc into a great lake. There it lay for a hundred years or more until another Head Druid in time of need, recovered it. Ever since then it has been used only sparingly to protect the Truth. But it is a dangerous thing that can eat away the soul of any adept who becomes too fond of its power, even you Alwyn, who may be the most powerful ever to wear it are not immune from its dangers!'

The listening Druids and the two warriors all shivered at this tale of ancient malevolence. It was Owain who broke the silence. 'Whilst I would sooner throw it to the bottom of the ocean here and now, I recognise that this Torc has helped save us more than once and so it must be kept. Perhaps it would be best kept by me. I am adept at nothing in your world so it has no pull for me. What do you say?'

The others, including Lorchar seemed relieved at this solution and agreed immediately. The Captain was by now anxious to complete the journey so they soon began to sail on towards Erin.

In due course, just as the sun was getting low in the western sky, on of the sailors in the bow of the ship cried out that he spied land. They sailed nearer and nearer the great green and grey mass of the Isle of Erin, with a stunning red and gold sky above it. Soon they could make out a pale beach with a green field raised above it. Beach and field were thronged with people. Nearer still and the excited travellers could make out men in rich clothes seated on golden chairs in the field. A sailor who came from Erin gasped as they beached the ship, and pointed at the group seated above.

'Up there the man with gold band round his head is Nial, High King of Erin and by his side on the left is Porit, King of Leinster, the man on his right in the long green robes and the bronze circlet must be the new Head Druid of Erin, you must indeed be illustrious guests!'

Now they could see faces and it was Pered's keen eyes that spotted that the man with green robes was familiar to them.

'Why that is our old friend Machan, is he now the Head Druid of all Erin?'

As the two parties approached each other on the beach and a man who was clearly a court Druid bustled forward self importantly to effect the introductions, Alwyn felt a sensation of great peace and happiness come over him, and in his head he heard a familiar voice say to him 'Well done Alwyn! You completed my task, well done to you all!'

Myrthin, it was his voice, so clearly did he hear it that he whirled around, half expecting to see the man himself. Of course he was not there. At first Alwyn was disappointed, but then he looked at the others, all of them were smiling, Branwen and Lorchar were in tears and Owain just looked shocked. In that moment Alwyn knew it, he did not know how and he did not know where, but he knew, with absolute certainty, Myrthin was alive!